```
F-W     Flynn, T.T.
Fly     Gunsmoke
```

DATE DUE

GUNSMOKE

GUNSMOKE

A WESTERN QUARTET

T. T. FLYNN

FIVE STAR

An imprint of Thomson Gale, a part of The Thomson Corporation

THOMSON

™

GALE

Detroit • New York • San Francisco • New Haven, Conn. • Waterville, Maine • London

LIBRARY OF CONGRESS CATALOGING-IN-PUBLICATION DATA

Flynn, T. T.
    Gunsmoke : a western quartet / by T.T. Flynn. — 1st ed.
      p. cm. — (A Five Star western)
    ISBN-13: 978-1-59414-559-9 (alk. paper)
    ISBN-10: 1-59414-559-8 (alk. paper)
    I. Title.
PS3556.L93G86 2007
813'.54—dc22
                            2007012041

First Edition. First Printing: September 2007.

Published in 2007 in conjunction with Golden West Literary Agency.

Printed in the United States of America on permanent paper
10 9 8 7 6 5 4 3 2 1

CONTENTS

★ ★ ★ ★ ★

DEAD MAN DEPUTY

★ ★ ★ ★ ★

T. T. Flynn did not title this story when he finished it in early February, 1940. It was one of several short novels that his agent, Marguerite E. Harper, had pre-sold in advance of being written to Street & Smith's *Western Story*. His agent sent it in at once to John Burr, editor of the magazine who very much wanted fiction in the magazine by Harper's leading clients, T. T. Flynn, Peter Dawson, and Luke Short. The author was paid $341.16. The story was titled "Dead Man Deputy" when it appeared in the issue dated January 4, 1941.

I

Old Buckshot Bledsoe knew he stood out in this gay fandango crowd like a wart on a Chihuahua *señorita*'s nose. His greasy leather breeches, scuffed rawhide coat, and ragged, grizzled whiskers were a sorry sight beside the strutting officers of the local garrison.

Buckshot's long nose twitched like an ancient hound dog testing the wind as he gripped the old rifle tighter and edged through the talk and laughter, the music and shuffle of dancing feet, the sour-sweet smell of *pulque* and odors of tequila, aguardiente, fancy powders, perfumes, and rank black-tobacco cigarettes.

Dust and dirt from the hard trail helped make a man look like a *pelado* among these women all painted and powdered, in fine dresses, with graceful *mantillas* draped from high combs. There had been nothing like this in the sun-blasted cactus country and rugged mountains stretching north to the border. And there was nothing like this north of the border either, where fear stalked the San Angelo range and Lindy Lou Merriman rode, pale and proud, past the jeering smiles of range riffraff that swaggered in the dusty San Angelo plaza.

Buckshot breathed it in. The music did kind of get in your blood after the past grim months when each rising sun brought threat and trouble. A man sort of forgot there was music and laughter in the world, and men and women who had no thought of the morrow and what it might bring.

Unconsciously Buckshot caught the dance rhythm and tapped the floor with a worn moccasin sole as he peered around and swore impatiently under his breath. Where in forty blue devils was a blue-eyed *gringo* who looked like a Mexican? Whose right cheek was badly scarred and whose twisted smile men remembered and women cherished.

Ponchito, the natives called him—Little Mild One. And Ponchito's six feet of height had nothing to do with the name. They'd tell you of gunfights he'd had, of men his guns had killed, that tall, blue-eyed *gringo* who rode with sadness behind laughter, and had kindness for honest peons.

"Triste," more than one peon's woman had described the man along the hard trail Buckshot's patience had unraveled. *"Sí, muy triste."*

"Sad, very sad," they had said, those black-eyed, soft-voiced native women who had looked into Ponchito's twisted merry smile. They had sensed a lurking sadness as women sense many things concerning men. And little would they say. You could feel their thoughts as they shrugged with polite vagueness. Why should a *gringo* stranger be following Ponchito, whose friends had no need to ask questions. Strangers riding in from the horizons and asking questions that might mean harm to Ponchito.

Here in Zamora, at the *cantina* of the Red Parrot, the fat old woman with the faint dark mustache on her upper lip had shrugged when Ponchito's name was mentioned and said with a rolling of eyes that tonight all *caballeros* were at the dance.

Now Buckshot snorted to himself. The *caballeros* were here all right—and who'd ever look for Jim Tennant hoorawing with these slicked-up Mexes? Not the Jim Tennant that Buckshot Bledsoe and Lindy Lou Merriman had known. Nobody here even looked like that kid, Jim.

That wasn't the first time Buckshot had had doubts on the

long trail south. Jim Tennant was probably dead after all. You couldn't bring a man back with a hunch—and a hunch was all that had started this trip.

Buckshot stopped, staring—rising on his toes to see better. Then his whoop rang out above all the fandango gaiety.

"Jim! Jim Tennant!" Elbowing, pushing, Buckshot plowed across the dance floor. "Here, Jim! It's Buckshot! I've been huntin' you from hell to breakfast!"

A dapper young Mexican got in the way. Buckshot elbowed him aside and plowed on toward the tall, scar-cheeked young man in silver-braided *charro* clothes who had turned quickly from a pretty *señorita*.

The man didn't look like the Jim Tennant that Buckshot had known. He looked taller, broader, older. Older in his face, older inside. You could sense it before you could explain why, but Buckshot's shout of delight was loud with certainty.

"You're a 'coon in that get-up, Jim! Holy smokes, you look like the head Mex of the town!"

A mustached officer of dragoons, fat, fierce, scowling in his gold-braided uniform, caught Buckshot by the arm and exploded in furious Spanish. "Burro! Son-of-a-dog! Get out!"

Buckshot moved in the worn moccasins like a rangy old cat. "Who you pawin', feller? Git back afore I git mad!"

A push with the rifle drove the officer back, tripping, floundering on the floor among the dancers. A girl screamed and other women cried out as a flurry of panic spread from the spot.

The fat officer cried out angrily as he was helped up. But Buckshot ignored all that as he reached his man and grabbed a sinewy hand.

"I ain't hardly believin' it, Jim! Chuck all this hoorawin' an' let's git where we can talk!"

Close up you could see that the young *charro*'s eyes were

blue in a saddle-covered face. The right cheek had been laid open savagely sometime in the past, and imperfectly healed, so that the face looked different and the mouth corner would twist slightly with wry humor when a smile started.

But there had been no smile when Buckshot's yell rang through the fandango hall. The dark, scarred face had turned with startled attention. A frown had followed as Buckshot burst through the dancers. Now the face was blank, revealing nothing as Buckshot caught the sinewy hand.

Buckshot had no thought of the people behind them. The shrill voices of excited women were dying away as the women began edging off the dance floor. Men, vociferous and angry, were gathering around the heavy dragoon officer whose dignity had been so rudely upset.

The *señorita* put her hand with a frightened gesture on the tall *charro*'s arm. She was an eyeful, Buckshot noticed, with red lips, dark, soft eyes, young and slender under the high tortoise-shell comb and graceful *mantilla*.

"This man . . . who is he?" she questioned uneasily in Spanish. "Chavez will have his life!"

Buckshot ignored her as he dropped the sinewy hand. His voice changed.

"That face don't fool me, Jim. If you don't keer to know me, speak up an' say so. If Lindy Lou Merriman bein' in trouble don't mean anythin' to you, I'll be gittin' back to the border." He finished with a quick snort of disappointment. "I never figured you'd turn Mex all the way through."

Something happened to that scarred face. A tightening of muscles, a sudden hard alertness and interest that might mean anything. So might the tall young man's sharp question in English mean anything.

"Lindy Lou's in trouble?"

"Plenty trouble."

"Did she send you here?"

"Hell, no! Like all the rest, Lindy Lou figures you're dead."

The twisted smile was an abrupt reality, coming quickly, vanishing almost as quickly, as if a fence of reserve had broken and a quick decision had been made. The young *charro* spoke to the girl swiftly in Spanish.

"Go with God, *amigita*. I must go."

"Go, Antonio? Where?"

"*¿Quién sabe?*" He shrugged at the dismay in her face—and with a snap of urgency spoke to Buckshot. "Jump fast, you bat-eared old hellion. You've raised more dust here than we can settle. Colonel Chavez runs these parts with hellfire and murder. Get to one of the back windows!"

Buckshot's grizzled whiskers split in a delighted grin and a whoop.

"I knowed you wasn't like that! Bring on your Mexes! I can handle ary one er all!" He turned to yell defiance at anyone who wanted trouble—and Jim Tennant's hand knocked him staggeringly aside an instant before a hard-thrown knife buried itself in Buckshot's left shoulder.

Swearing as he reached back to jerk out the knife, Buckshot had his first good look at the man the natives called Ponchito— Little Mild One. And by all the signs that a man could trust this man was not Jim Tennant. Not the grinning, friendly, young fellow the San Angelo country had known. The twisted smile was close to being savage, in a way the old Jim Tennant could never have been. And a gun whipping out from under the *charro* jacket crashed a shot at the ceiling in equally savage warning.

The fat Chavez, evidently commanding the local garrison, had bawled commands to willing ears. The fandango hall was like a rudely kicked hornet's nest, men shouting, surging forward, and others coming behind them. Shoot one, and two more would take his place.

Buckshot yelled at them, clubbing the heavy rifle as he charged toward the back windows. The dance had dissolved into a mêlée of screaming women, shouting, pushing men, knives flashing here and there, and several guns blasting shots into the ceiling. It would have been worse, Buckshot guessed as he swung the rifle furiously, if most of the men hadn't come without knives or guns.

A hand grabbed at Buckshot's injured shoulder. He raked at it with the knife he'd torn from the shoulder muscles. The hand pulled away—and the clubbed rifle stock smashed a looming, mustached face. The nose crushed flat and the face went back and down.

Then a raking knife slashed Buckshot's rawhide coat and the flesh underneath. No time to yell now or swear. Little room to swing the rifle. Buckshot snatched for his holstered belt gun and shot the man at his side before the knife could slash again.

The roaring gun blast stopped the nearest men like the blow of an invisible hand. They crowded back on the others behind them while Buckshot charged to the nearest window.

Lights had been shot out, put out, smashed out back in the big hall. In semidarkness Buckshot turned at bay before the window and saw the tall young *charro* at his heels.

"Jump quick!" the *charro* cried.

Buckshot went through the open window in a scrambling, headlong dive. He struck the ground hard in the darkness and rolled in dirt and dust. A figure landed hard beside him a moment later and stumbled over him.

"Buckshot!"

"*Arghhhh!*" Buckshot came up spitting dust and still clutching the rifle and hand gun. "Enough dirt in my damn' whiskers to grow chiles. Them damn' Mexes is like wildcats in a barrel. Wait'll I clean 'em outta that window."

Jim Tennant caught his arm in the darkness.

14

"Never mind that. It won't help. Make it worse. This way. Where's your horse?"

"Out front."

"You'll never get him now. Chavez will have men out there already."

The black night gave them cover. Jim led the way at a run along what seemed to be a dusty, smelly little alley. The tumult back at the fandango hall faded. For the moment anyway no one seemed to be following them along the alley.

"I'd like to git that Chavez myself," Buckshot panted, slapping dust out of his whiskers.

"Chavez'll have your hide in strips," was the harsh panting answer as they ran. "These aren't border Mexicans ducking trouble with a *gringo*. Chavez is a bad *hombre*. *Muy malo*. His men are worse. You surprised them. We had plenty luck getting to a window. But it won't last. Run, you old brush popper . . . while you've got a chance!"

Jim Tennant knew the dark alleys of Zamora like a native. They turned right, then left, crossed a narrow street, plunged into another alley, made another turn, and finally shouldered into a low-roofed adobe stable where horses stamped and nickered at their coming and Jim Tennant's low call of: "Pablo?"

"*Sí, señor*," came back out of the darkness.

"My horse. Two horses quick." And in English, Jim Tennant said: "Help him, Buckshot. I'll be back in a minute. Don't make any noise."

That was the way they left the stable a few minutes later, hurriedly, furtively—but at the second corner where they turned a shout rang out behind them. A rifle report drove lead viciously past Buckshot's ear.

15

II

Jim spurred into a gallop down the narrow, dusty street. The town had been seething with voices and movement when they rode away from the stable. Now other shots and warning shouts came from a dozen points. Pursuit sprang up after them like a scattered hunting pack converging on a hot trail.

They raced out of town by a different road than Buckshot had entered on—a road leading southwest, as near as Buckshot could judge—and the first riders were not far behind them. Cold water splashed high as they galloped through a shallow, brawling little stream just beyond town. A mile or so farther on, in broken, brushy foothills, Jim swerved suddenly to the right, up through the brush of a rising draw.

A turn put them out of sight of the road, and Jim reined up. When he spoke, his voice was soberly calm.

"Maybe it'll work. I've had this way picked out since last year in case I ever had to make a run for it. Never knew how far I could trust Chavez. If they come after us, get ready to ride an' fight. They know this kind of work."

Moments later the drumming rush of pursuit reached the point where the draw crossed the road—and swept past without slackening. A half dozen—a dozen riders and more—strung out, riding furiously.

Jim waited a little and then, looking at Buckshot, laughed softly.

"That'll hold 'em for a little. There's a trail ahead that'll swing us around to the north and set us toward the border. After Chavez thinks twice, he'll know we're cutting around that way and he'll be after us. If we're lucky, we'll get through. If we aren't, he'll have us. Save a bullet for yourself. It'll be easier."

Buckshot snorted. "Plenty bad *hombre*, huh?"

"Plenty bad on his own range or off," Jim agreed, sober once more. "And worse on his range. There's things I've turned up

16

lately about him that'd get him shot if Mexico City knew about it all. Now then, where'd you come from? How'd you know I was at that dance?"

"I been everywhere else," Buckshot said tartly. "Two weeks I been trailin' around tryin' to ketch up with a scar-cheeked feller called Ponchito that I hear talked about some along the border. A young *gringo* that had turned Mex, they said, and had kilt him no end of hardcases that was livin' off gun play and makin' trouble for honest folks."

"So you found Ponchito . . . and saw he looked like Jim Tennant?"

"Holy mackerel, no!" Buckshot said quickly. "When I heerd about the scar, I had me a crazy idea this Ponchito might be you, Jim. The last look Hacksaw Jones had at you in that Antelope Cañon fight, you was layin' on the floor of that old adobe barn with your face all laid open where a bullet had glanced off somethin' an' tore up your cheek. Then they fired the barn and Hacksaw tried a run fer the open. They shot him in the leg and brought him down. And Bull Merriman and Henry Clarkson an' their gunmen come up close an' watched the barn burn down over what was inside."

"It made a fire, too." Jim's voice was bleak. "Old hay was still stored in the top."

"I reckon," Buckshot agreed. "I heerd Merriman's men and them Ladrone Cattle Company gunmen that was with 'em talkin' about the way the fire roared when she busted good through the roof. Next mornin' when the ashes was cool enough to git the bodies out, they found one body holdin' your gun. Them fancy silver spurs you owned was in a pocket. They figured that was enough an' buried the body under your name." Buckshot chuckled under his breath. "The buryin' was done in town. Old Bull Merriman swore he wouldn't have no yaller, thievin', murderin' trash planted under his land and grass. I was

17

at the funeral and listened to your friends and the rest havin' their last say. It must've made your ears burn, Jim."

"I'll bet," the other said dryly. "What happened to Hacksaw?"

"Bull Merriman got law righteous and turned Hack over to the sheriff. Hack's shot leg got blood poisoning and kilt him in two, three days. But I seen Hack right after they throwed him in jail. He said he guessed you never felt the fire, seein' as how you looked when he run out. Your cheek all tore open an' no doubt you was good as dead then." Buckshot spat in the darkness. "I seen the body they took outta the ashes. Wasn't a man there could've been sure who it was after the fire had cooled off. But both cheeks showed that no bullets had opened 'em like Hack swore had happened."

"Who heard Hack tell that and got a look at the body like you did?" Jim asked sharply.

"Nobody, I reckon. Hack promised he wouldn't say nothin'. He died mighty fast after that. I never told it, Jim. But since then I've wondered plenty if you really was kilt that night . . . and how in Hades you got outta that burning barn if you did get out."

"How could I have gotten out if they buried me?"

"Maybe you stayed right there an' died after all, damn it!" Buckshot said acidly.

"That's what happened."

"I'm talkin' sense, Jim!"

"So am I," was the dry answer. "Jim Tennant died right there in the barn when the roof and that burning hay fell down. Died, I tell you. No one's heard of him or seen him around since then, have they?" And more lightly Jim said: "I wondered where those silver spurs went. A fellow with us who called himself Slim Tom liked their looks. He must have grabbed them the first chance he got. And did me a mighty good turn when he did. He helped kill off Jim Tennant and get him buried."

"No man ever died deader around San Angelo than Jim Tennant after they found them spurs," Buckshot agreed. "Suits me, son, if it suits you. If I hadn't come lookin' for you to maybe be alive, I wouldn't have knowed you myself, what with that Mex look about you and your face all changed."

"The fire scorched me up pretty bad," Jim explained soberly. "I got down the cañon a couple of miles, near out of my head, and run into that 'breed herb man, Wild Horse Joe, who hung out around Ladrone Mountain. Joe had been out skulking around and saw the fire. He piled me on his horse, got me over on Ladrone Mountain, the other side of Clarkson's west pasture, and used Indian medicine on me. I never knew what it was but it worked pretty well. The skin drew up some around the scar, so I didn't look so good. But I had a face left and I was satisfied."

"You look nigh as good, only different. It ain't all around that scar, either," Buckshot said shrewdly. "It's inside, too. You ain't the same feller inside, Jim. And it shows outside."

Jim said nothing to that. He reined up and listened. They were on higher ground. Far off to the right a few little twinkling lights marked part of the town they'd left. The scrub brush around them was quiet and the back trail was quiet, too.

As they rode on along the rough, narrow trail, Jim said soberly: "Maybe you're right, Buckshot. I've changed. Bull Merriman did it when he made me out a killer and a thief and had me shot down and burned up and buried back there in San Angelo. I wasn't much more than a kid, trying to do the right thing. I was there at Antelope Cañon trying to find who had cleaned out my little bunch of stock and was cleaning out the other ranchers. And Bull Merriman caught us in a trap. Him and Clarkson's gunmen. One of the men with us must have been working with them. Anyway, I changed after they killed Jim Tennant and buried him."

"Makes me feel like I'm ridin' with a corpse," Buckshot complained. "If you're dead, then who the devil are you now?"

"The *Mejicanos* across the border treated me white when I showed up among them, busted, sick, and still half crippled from a bullet through my ribs. The poorer the *Mejicano,* the better he and his family treated me. They were the kind of folks I was hungry for. The kind who wouldn't do you dirt when you tried to help them. I'd left Jim Tennant buried back in San Angelo. So I picked a name I heard one of the women calling me and made it Antonio Ponchito y Río. It was as good as any. It fitted in the way I was living. It's done all right."

"You picked a mouthful," Buckshot commented. "Tony, huh . . . an' your mother's family name was Ponchito and your father's name was the river."

"*Sí, señor.* And now . . . what about Lindy Lou?"

"*Muy malo,*" Buckshot said, and grumbled: "You're gettin' me thinkin' Mex, too! Ain't you heard how things has gone around San Angelo?"

"Never heard much. Never wanted to after I walked across the border. It's been almost five years. Bull Merriman's still Bull Merriman, I suppose. And Lindy Lou's married like Bull wanted her to, and has a couple of kids, maybe?"

"Maybe you're married, too?" Buckshot countered.

"No."

"Then you know dog-gone well Lindy Lou ain't," snorted Buckshot. "Leastways you hoped not. When you heard Lindy Lou's name, you forgot that pretty face at the dance there with you . . . an' everything else."

"I had to get you out before Chavez and his men cornered you."

"An' old brush tick like me never made no man leave a pretty gal," Buckshot stated shrewdly. "Bull Merriman's dead, Jim. Lindy Lou ain't married . . . an' San Angelo has gone to hell.

Complete an' glory-busted hell!"

"Merriman's dead?"

"Shot in the back on the Ojo Caliente trail last fall." Buckshot's voice took on a grim edge of humor. "Bull's buried in the San Angelo buryin' ground, right up the slope from you. When the dark of the moon comes an' the ghosts start walkin', you two prob'ly raise Ned with each other all over the graves."

Jim Tennant did not laugh. "Lindy Lou owns the ranch then?"

"What's left of it," answered Buckshot. "The Merriman Hook 'n' Ladder brand is picked cleaner than a coyote-killed sheep. Henry Clarkson's Ladrone Land and Cattle Company is all that's sittin' purty. And Henry Clarkson. Other folks is like Bull Merriman's outfit. Hard times. Decent folks afraid. Hardcases ridin' high. And no doubt about what's behind it. Henry Clarkson's behind it."

"Never thought I'd hear that," Jim muttered. "Clarkson was thick with Lindy Lou's father. He was courtin' Lindy Lou, with Bull egging it on and Lindy Lou pretty cold to me after her brother was killed."

"Bull and Lindy Lou both knowed different before Bull died," Buckshot told him. "So did a heap of others who'd hung out a welcome sign when Henry Clarkson showed up with cash money and talked old man Riggins an' Tom Dirk into puttin' their land an' Clarkson's money into the Ladrone Cattle Company." On the dark trail behind Jim Tennant, Buckshot stopped speaking to snort his disgust before he continued. "It sounded good. Henry Clarkson talked loud how he had cash money that was hungry to be workin'. Riggins and Dirk had plenty of land that wasn't doin' them much good what with border jumpers hazing off most of their stock. Clarkson said his money'd put cattle back on the land an' hire gunmen to keep 'em safe. Maybe you remember all that, Jim? How Clarkson swore in public nary a cow er steer'd be rustled off Ladrone land if he had to hire a gunman fer every cow."

"I remember," was the grim reply. "Clarkson kept his word. He brought in cattle, and gunmen to watch them. And after that rustlers seemed to be leaving the new Ladrone range alone and going after little outfits like the one I had after I quit riding for Bull Merriman."

"Uhn-huh," Buckshot agreed. "And the cattle an' the gunmen stayed on Clarkson's land. Gunmen that'd make ary good sheriff bristle when he got downwind from one. Strangers comin' an' goin' from that Ladrone outfit . . . an' all the time rustlers cleanin' out other parts of the range. Clarkson fooled them all, Jim! Bull Merriman, too. They see it now. Maybe Clarkson never had that cash money. Nobody seen much of it. Clarkson talked hisself into part title on that Riggins an' Dirk land. He said he paid for the cattle that was trailed north acrost the border to stock the place. Chances are, if he paid, he took it from one pocket an' put it in the other.

"An' then Clarkson set tight with his cattle an' gunmen while the rest of the range bled to death. And for every dollar someone else lost, another dollar got in Henry Clarkson's pocket. You couldn't prove it. You couldn't notice it at first. Clarkson said he'd bring in gunmen an' he did. Said he'd keep his Ladrone outfit fat and safe . . . an' he did. Folks at first didn't look for the Ladrone gunmen to have any connection with other troubles . . . Clarkson had brought the gunmen in to keep trouble away. You see how easy it was, Jim?"

"Makes a pretty plain trail," admitted Tennant.

"Folks couldn't see it at first," Buckshot said harshly. "Henry Clarkson got hisself a ranch fer talk an' nothing else . . . an' then kept open house fer gunmen an' trouble right under everybody's nose. An' they liked him for it an' cheered him on at first. No wonder he kept a greasy smile on that meaty face o' his. He was laughin' at them and they didn't know it. An' when they did know, it was too late to do much. Things had a way of happening to folks that talked out and tried to git somethin' done about it."

"Like Bull Merriman getting shot?"

"Like that . . . and like Bull's boy, Rolf, that you got blamed for killing," Buckshot said. "Folks that cross Henry Clarkson get in trouble. You crossed him plenty on account of Lindy Lou. So Lindy Lou's brother got kilt. It looked like you done it. They couldn't prove it in court. But Bull Merriman hated your guts after that, an' things wasn't the same between you and Lindy Lou. I remember. I've thought a heap about it. They couldn't prove you kilt Rolf Merriman . . . but there wasn't no way fer you to prove you didn't kill him. An' it helped Henry Clarkson plenty in his courtin'."

"Did it?" Jim asked slowly.

"It kept you away from the Hook 'n' Ladder," Buckshot pointed out. "It turned Bull Merriman against you. Wasn't long before your little spread was cleaned an' you was trapped in Antelope Cañon an' shot an' buried. Which gave Henry Clarkson open range with Lindy Lou." The old man shook his head. "It wasn't all clear, then, boy. You can look back now an' see it. An' then, when Bull Merriman's turn came, he got put outta the way, too."

"Because Lindy Lou wouldn't marry Clarkson?"

"Turn up your own cards on that, son. But the San Angelo range is in Henry Clarkson's pocket now. Sheriff an' all. Lindy Lou is hangin' onto the Hook 'n' Ladder with nothin' much to hang to. And fast as ary man gits his head up where he might make trouble for Clarkson, his head gits took off. It was watchin' Lindy Lou facin' it alone set me thinkin' hard about you, Jim. So I took me a *pasear* down this way to see if you might maybe be alive after all . . . an' still remembered Lindy Lou."

"What happened to Tom Dirk and old man Riggins?"

"Tom Dirk didn't like the way things was goin' under Clarkson's orders and said so," Buckshot answered dryly. "One day his horse throwed him an' busted his head open on a rock. Leastways the Clarkson men who found him said that's what happened. Dirk's head was busted anyway. And Clarkson had notes showin' that Dirk owed him most of his share in the ranch. Wasn't no relatives to argue about it."

"Old man Riggins have an accident, too?"

"Nope," said Buckshot. "When Dirk got kilt, Riggins moved quick to El Paso. I hear he don't get much outta his share of the ranch now. But at least he don't fall off horses an' he ain't been shot in the back yet. Riggins stays drunk most of the time, cussin' himself for a fool in puttin' a snake like Clarkson inside his shirt when he was cold sober. Ed Lawlor talked to the old man in El Paso two, three months. . . ."

Buckshot broke off as his horse nickered loudly. Off to the right, in the direction of those last seen feeble lights of town, a shout challenged the night.

"*¿Quién es?*"

"More of them coming to block this trail!" Jim whipped back over his shoulder. "It'll be a run now! Stay with me!"

The challenge came again as they spurred into a reckless gallop on the rough trail. A shout and a burst of warning shots announced their discovery, then it was another race through blackness and unfamiliar country where a stranger like Buckshot would have been confused, baffled on the haphazard trails that had no direction or meaning in the night.

Jim seemed to know where he was going. His hard-running horse plunged through low hills that grew more broken and rough, with the way twisting, turning, now up, now down, until one steep down trail took them toward the lower valley lands well north of town. And when Tennant pulled up his blowing horse, a distant shout and its answer were far behind.

"Looked like we were riding for the mountains over there to the west," Jim said calmly. "That'll hold 'em for a little if Chavez hasn't got the valley cut off already. Let's go."

It was a ride. Buckshot was tough, but his eyes were red with weariness and the horses were dead beat when another trail brought them over mountains far to the northeast and the way dropped down for miles through the cool, bright dawn.

Pursuit had long vanished behind them but Jim's face wore a grim expression.

"They'll keep coming after they figure out our trail. Chavez don't keep men around who give up. Friend of mine down at the foot of the mountain has a few horses. I did him a favor once. He'll give us fresh mounts. We've got to keep ahead all day if you can burr on."

"I can stay with ary man!" retorted Buckshot.

But when the long hot day brought them at dusk to small adobe ranch buildings far out in the dry country toward the border, Buckshot staggered with weariness when he climbed off the drooping horse.

"I got to rest here tonight if it means fightin' forty of them Chavez men fer it," he groaned.

Jim, too, was haggard and dusty. Cheek bones looked sharper and a gaunt, fierce look seemed to have settled like a mask on his face. But the twisted smile came with his nod.

"Sleep and eat hearty, and then head for San Angelo. I'll be gone when you get up."

Startled, Buckshot threw him a challenging look. "Ain't you comin' acrost the border? Ain't you comin' to San Angelo?"

"Maybe," Jim said enigmatically. "But if we meet, *amigo*, I'll do first talking. You never saw me. I'm still dead. Savvy?"

"*Sí*," Buckshot said mechanically. Then he groaned. "Hell, no, I don't savvy. But I'm too beat out to argy. Gimme a corner to fall in an' sleep."

III

The border was a day's ride south of San Angelo. Mountains loomed southwest and on the northern horizon. The range was rolling, studded with hills, rough in many places, with cañons and narrow valleys south along the border.

San Angelo had not changed much. The graveyard still looked the same with mounds and crosses behind the unpainted picket fence on higher ground along the El Paso road. The trail-dusty rider in Mexican dress who rode along singing under his breath in the afternoon sun broke off to salute the graveyard and smile faintly as he passed. He was humming to himself as he jogged on into town.

The tall cottonwoods still grew by the shallows of Angel Creek. The low adobe houses on the edge of town were still the same. Children shrilled, dogs barked, Mexican men and women stared admiringly as the *caballero* passed.

Few men like this rode north of the border. Tall young men in tight *charro* breeches, snug silver-braided jackets, silver spurs and silver-mounted bridles, costly saddles and gun holsters. He would furnish material for conversation in the little adobe houses tonight and in the saloons and the stores around the dusty plaza. Jim Tennant smiled a little at the thought, but the blue eyes in his dark face were sharp and thoughtful as he rode into the plaza.

Not much difference here at first sight, either. Wagons and saddle horses were at the hitch racks. Men loitered before the buildings—cowmen, Mexicans, a booted man or two in from the nearby mountains where the small mines and prospectors were always busy. Plenty of life, even at this time of day.

The same—and yet there was a difference when Jim recalled memories of the plaza four years back. Most of the loiterers looked harder, rougher. Strange faces, strange men who eyed a newcomer with cold wariness seldom seen back when Jim Ten-

26

nant was buried beside the El Paso road.

A jeer came from one group as the black horse drew abreast.

"Bug your eyes, boys," a stocky man with a red beard stubble jeered. "Ain't he a dude? Bet the drinks I can put lead through his hat an' touch nary a hair."

The shot crashed as the words ended. Jim's peaked Mexican sombrero jerked as a bullet tore through the crown.

Jim reined up and removed the sombrero without looking around. The crown was holed at the top. Scant inches lower, the bullet would have killed the wearer.

A hush had fallen over the plaza as those in the open turned to watch, and others hurried out of doorways.

Jim reined the black horse back to the four idlers before the saloon. The short, stocky man who had jeered and fired the shot was standing there with the gun cocked and a hard grin behind the reddish stubble on his face.

"How's my shootin', Alex?"

An exploring finger showed white through the holes in the hat, and a chuckle followed as the finger came out. " '*Sta bueno, amigo.* W'at you say . . . good?"

"You're damned right it's good! Put 'er on again an' I'll open them holes some more."

White teeth showed in another chuckle. "Es treek, no? You savvy?" Thumb and forefinger fished a silver *peso* out of the *charro* jacket and flipped the coin in the air. The same hand made a fast gun draw that looked almost casual and a bullet drove the falling *peso* far out into the plaza.

"There's a trick for you, Red!" a bearded man beside the stocky gunman chortled. "How'll you bet the drinks on tryin' that?"

Smiling, Jim fished out another *peso* to flip. But Red grinned sheepishly and holstered his gun.

"I know when I'm licked. Ride on, stranger. You're good in

27

any man's town."

"*Gracias, señor. Señor* Clarkson . . . w'ere I fin'?"

"Henry Clarkson?"

"*Sí.*"

"Try the bank. He's mostly there afternoons."

"*¿Banco?*"

"Over there. That brick building," Red said, pointing.

"*Gracias.*"

Jim turned the black horse across the plaza, humming under his breath. Behind him remarks were audible:

"Wonder who'n hell he is?"

"Some of Clarkson's business, I reckon."

"He shore showed you up, Red."

Only the gold lettering on the front door of the small brick bank building had changed, Jim discovered. It now read: *Henry Clarkson, President.*

Ike Blodgett, behind the iron grille work, seemed to be wearing the same black sleeve guards, old eyeshade, and pen behind his ear as his bony fingers stacked silver dollars.

"*Buenos días, señor.*"

The cashier looked bleakly through the grille work. "Howdy, mister. What'll it be?"

"*Señor* Clarkson?"

"He's busy. What is it?"

"No spik Engleesh."

"You're outta luck then," Ike said shortly. "You savvy Clarkson busy? Woman . . . *mujer* . . . Clarkson, busy. *Mucho* busy."

The stranger grinned and nodded. "*Sí, sí, Señor* Clarkson's *mujer,* she's busy?"

"Not that. You'll have to wait. Savvy wait?" Ike's sharp face was frowning as he stared through the grille work. "Seems like I've seen you somewhere," he said dubiously.

The stranger smiled politely—a twisted, queer smile—and

started to roll a cigarette. And just then the door of the bank president's office at the back opened and let out a man's voice hearty with assurance.

"Any time you need money it's here. We're glad to let you have it."

A woman's voice answered. "I know how my credit stands here. Put the money in my account and I'll pay what I can on the other notes as. . . ."

Jim Tennant stiffened at the sound of her voice. Then she was in the doorway, head high, angry color in her cheeks. She saw him shaping the cigarette and the catch of her breath stopped her words.

"This fellow's to see you, Mister Clarkson!" Ike Blodgett called. "He don't savvy English. You'll have to handle him."

Jim Tennant put the cigarette between his lips and scratched a match with his thumbnail. Lindy Lou Merriman hadn't changed. A little older, like himself. And prettier for it, with a breath of the open range clean and heady about her. And her share of stubborn pride, like Bull Merriman, who'd known he was better than most men and shown it. But still Lindy Lou, whose clear voice and laughter had stayed with Jim through a thousand nights of strange faces and strange country.

Lindy Lou had paled. Her look was stunned, questioning. And when Ike Blodgett spoke, she swallowed and walked blindly past Jim's carefully blank look and out of the bank.

Henry Clarkson's eyes followed her out of sight before they went to the visitor.

Years back Clarkson's face had been broad and pink, with too many loud laughs always on tap when needed. Now the man was fat, puffy about the eyes, and the mouth was loose and greedy, as Lindy Lou walked out of the bank. Clarkson stood for a moment more in thought that made him smile with some inner satisfaction. Then he turned with a plump hand outstretched and a greeting in fair Spanish.

"*Buenas tardes.* What is it?"

"*Señor* Clarkson?"

"Yes."

"I have to talk with you."

Clarkson's look suddenly narrowed. He started to say something, changed his mind, motioned to the office. "Come in and talk."

The wary scrutiny of the plaza idlers was in the banker's manner as they entered the office. "Do I know you?" Clarkson questioned.

Jim pulled off the big sombrero and bowed.

"*Señor,* I am *Don* Antonio Ponchito y Río. To see you is one happy moment."

Clarkson motioned to a chair. "You reminded me of someone for a minute," he grunted. "He'd be about your age now if he hadn't been killed."

"Ah, so? A friend?"

"Not him. He was a killer and a thief and he was shot down rustling. What can I do for you, *Señor*"—Clarkson's voice changed—"Antonio Ponchito. Are you the one they call Ponchito down in Chihuahua and Sonora?" He shifted into English. "You must be. That one's got a scar on his cheek, too."

"*Sí, señor* Ponchito. You know Chihuahua and Sonora then? You know me?"

The desk chair *creaked* as Clarkson pulled it around and sat down heavily. His eyes had narrowed again.

"Maybe you want a job. I can always use a good gun hand if he'll take orders. Fifty a month and extra money when you earn it. How does that do?"

"Fifty *pesos?*" Jim chuckled. "*Señor,* I am worth more. Much more. I, *Don* Antonio Ponchito y Río, am owner of much land, much cattle. I, too, have many men work for me."

"That way, is it?" Clarkson said. "My mistake. Maybe you've got some cattle to sell then? Must be that, eh, to bring you up this way?"

"*Sí, señor.* Many cattle to sell . . . I hope."

"The price has to be right when I buy."

"And no questions asked, *señor,* they say?"

Clarkson shrugged. "We'll talk about that later if you mean business. Where are your cattle? How many for sale?"

"We will see how many." Jim chuckled. "You, *señor,* can tell me about my cattle and my land. Oh, *sí.* We own them together. I have bought from *Señor* Eduardo Riggins, in El Paso, one-third of this Ladrone Cattle Company. We own much cattle and land, you and I, *amigo,* eh?"

The fat face went expressionless as Henry Clarkson hunched in the desk chair. But his voice had a new edge.

"You bought out Riggins?" he questioned carefully.

"*Sí, señor.*"

"He wouldn't sell. Told me so."

"Ah, *señor,* to me he sell. You want the papers, no? A good lawyer made the papers. I have copies to show you. Here."

Clarkson read the documents his visitor handed over. He nodded and handed them back.

"Want to sell?"

"Why I sell? I have just bought. *Señor,* I have wanted the *hacienda* of my own. The cattle of my own. The men of my own. Now I have them. The lawyer comes to look at the books with me. We see what I buy, and then I, *Don* Antonio Ponchito y Río, will help with everything. No?"

"I'll pay a profit on your buy?"

"Ah, no . . . not for one thousand profits, *señor.* Tomorrow you will have the books? There will be many questions to ask."

Clarkson stirred. From somewhere his smile came back and he shrugged indifferently.

31

"All right. If you won't sell, you won't sell. The books are out at the ranch. Ride out there and make yourself at home. I'm an easy man to get along with. We'll do all right."

"*Gracias.* Perhaps tomorrow, *señor.* There is much to do. I wish to see everything. I will be busy, no? *Adiós.*"

The tall stranger was whistling jauntily as he walked out of the bank, past Ike Blodgett's thin face peering through the grille work. Ike's voice was brittle to the bank president, standing in the open doorway.

"He looks like that Tennant boy. Jim Tennant. Remember him?"

"Tennant's dead and buried," Clarkson said brusquely. "I'm going out. Won't be back today."

IV

In the next two hours San Angelo learned that Henry Clarkson had a new partner in the Ladrone Cattle Company. A partner for whom Clarkson hadn't asked and, it was said, didn't want.

Don Antonio Ponchito y Río told it himself, in Spanish and broken English, celebrating from bar to bar, while his Mexican gold and silver bought drinks for any man who was dry.

Buckshot Bledsoe in scuffed rawhide coat and buckskin breeches showed up after the second round of drinks and stayed grimly in the growing crowd, watching, listening, frowning now and then with growing displeasure

Red Carney took his share of drinks. He grinned thinly when the stranger showed the sombrero that his bullet had punctured, and spoke to him in Spanish.

Coly Johnson, one of Sheriff Lan Hanson's deputies, who understood Spanish, translated for Red. "He wants you workin' for the Ladrone outfit, Red. Says a man who can use a gun like you is a man after his own heart an' he wants you around. But not to shoot at his hat no more."

"Tell 'im he's hired a hand." Red grinned.

That made those within hearing laugh and it had to be explained to the stranger. Red Carney had been on the Ladrone payroll and Henry Clarkson had fired him.

The stranger laughed with the rest and said that Red was on the payroll again—this time for *Don* Antonio Ponchito y Río.

"I'll buy the drinks on that when I draw my first pay," Red said humorously, and this time no one explained the laughter that followed.

Long before the last drink was bought in the final saloon around the plaza, Jim Tennant saw men he had known in the old days. Men who eyed this dark, scar-cheeked stranger from across the border with furtive interest and spoke to one another, Buckshot Bledsoe included. After the last round of drinks, the stranger saluted them with—*"Adiós, amigos."*—and went off to the room he had hired in Joe Little's one-story adobe hotel on the corner of the plaza.

Fifteen minutes later Buckshot stopped outside the hotel room and heard a Mexican song inside. Buckshot was scowling as he tried the door, found it unlocked, and entered without knocking. He halted abruptly in mid-step before the cold threat of a gun muzzle.

Shaving lather covered half of Jim Tennant's face. A razor was in his other hand. He spoke in Spanish, grinning as he motioned with the gun for the door to be closed.

"Enter, *señor*. *Don* Antonio Ponchito y Río welcomes you."

"I'm glad to see you've got a little sense left anyway, havin' that gun ready," Buckshot blurted as he closed the door. "I knowed you was in town when Lindy Lou come by lookin' like a ghost an' said she'd seen a Mexican with a scar on his cheek who made her think of Jim Tennant." Buckshot glared. "What kinda foolishness is this?"

"You told her I was a fool?"

"I didn't tell her nothin'. I was ashamed to."

Jim chuckled as he put the gun by the crockery washbowl and answered in English.

"I wondered how long you'd go before busting out with it. In the Gunsight Bar you looked like something sour had lit in your whiskers and was tasting mighty bad."

"It ain't funny," Buckshot insisted. "What kinda fool trick is this, struttin' like a *fiesta* dude, an' tellin' the world you bought into partners with Clarkson? If it's a lie, Clarkson'll nail you quick fer it."

"It's gospel truth, *amigo*."

"Then it's a fool trick if I ever heerd or seen one," Buckshot said flatly. "Henry Clarkson wasn't in no hurry to get rid of old man Riggins. Things was running like he wanted. The old man didn't bother him none. Riggins couldn't even do nothing when Clarkson thieved most of the money the ranch made. And Riggins would've died or been killed off when Clarkson got around to it. Wasn't ary man in these parts, clean to El Paso, who'd 've throwed good money away by offering to buy the old man out."

"That's how Riggins seemed to figure when I talked to him in El Paso."

"So you really played the fool then? Give Riggins cash money? Where's your sense, boy? All them men takin' your drinks was laughin' at you. They knowed what a fool you was. They knowed Henry Clarkson'll git shut of you fast. While you was buyin' whiskey, they was layin' bets behind your back on how long you'd last. They figured old man Riggins was smart . . . an' this Mex, Ponchito, was plenty of a fool, even if he could shoot like slick lightnin'. Red Carney laughed when you hired him for the Ladrone. Red knowed he'd never draw pay money."

Jim chuckled. "That'll be twice Red didn't read the sign right. He'll have to do better for his pay."

Buckshot looked his disgust. "You fooled me, Jim. I thought

you was gonna ease back here an' do somethin' about Clarkson before he knowed what was happening. I figgered you was hard an' woolly. I thought you was the man to help some of us git our heads down to Clarkson an' his gunmen. I figgered you was one last chance to git this range back to the folks who usta own an' run it."

Jim finished the shaving and nodded as he wiped the razor. "I know, Buckshot."

"An' here you show up like a Fourth o' July parade!" Buckshot exploded. "You fix it so Clarkson'll have to have you killed, quick an' sure. An' on top of that you made out to hire the crookedest, cold-blooded, dirty-eyed snake anywhere along the border. Red Carney was too bad even fer Henry Clarkson."

Jim smiled as he reached for the towel.

"Red did sort of look tough and mean," he agreed. "But he called the cards on his shooting. Wasn't ashamed to come out second best. I cotton to a man who'll do that. Chances are he won't double-cross you to show how big he is. Hiring him'll make Clarkson show his hand that much faster."

"So you want to git killed fast?"

"I want Clarkson to make a move," asserted Jim. "He'll do it this way. He won't stand for a stranger riding in to help run things. He won't have another man asking questions and keeping an eye on his moves. And a Mexican at that."

"You bet he won't," Buckshot grunted. "An' buyin' drinks fer the town to celebrate only makes it worse."

Jim sat on the bed and grinned as he rolled a cigarette. "If I came back like I left, they'd start wondering fast if Jim Tennant was dead after all. A scar face don't change a man too much. They've already noticed I'm like Jim Tennant."

"More'n I thought they would," Buckskin admitted grudgingly.

"The law wanted Jim Tennant for rustling Ladrone and Hook

'n' Ladder beef," Jim continued. "The sheriff takes orders from Henry Clarkson. If they had an idea I was back, the law'd jump to lock me up. I'd have to fight and run. Maybe I wouldn't get the chance. The sheriff might shoot first. If I made it, I'd have to jump back across the border or hide out."

Buckskin nodded agreement to that.

"As it is, they've all got something else to think about," Jim pointed out. "Clarkson's got a partner to get rid of now. He's got to make his move first. He's on the wrong side of the law this time and folks are watching."

"Clarkson don't care who's watching."

Jim's grin had a hard edge. "He'll think about it. He's not dealing from a stacked deck now. He's crowded out in the open where everyone can watch his hand. And he don't like it. Over at the bank he looked like he'd grabbed a hot iron and didn't know what to do about it."

"He'll know what to do . . . an' he'll have it done! And what help'll you be dead to Lindy Lou, livin' out there on the dry bones of the Hook 'n' Ladder with only three hands workin' for her. The scrub beef that's left on Hook 'n' Ladder grass ain't worth a rustler's time. Borrowin' at the bank is all that's kept Lindy Lou an' the boys eatin' right. Fogey Wilson, Dan Coleman, an' old Rip Stevens has mighty near fergot what pay is. They're just stayin' around because it's Lindy Lou. Took Clarkson a long time . . . but he's got the Hook 'n' Ladder where he wants it. If he can't have Bull's girl, he'll git Bull's land. And what'll all this foolishness do to help after you're killed?"

Jim reached for his gun belt, hanging on the bedpost.

"I don't mean to die," he said flatly. "Down there across the border I've just been drifting. Never could find what I wanted. Saved money but there was nothing I wanted to do with it. I was a fool but it ain't too late. I know what I want. A ranch like I started to build after I quit Bull Merriman. I've got a toehold now. There's a tally to settle with Clarkson . . . and I'm close now where I can get at him."

"You mean where he can get at you," Buckshot said bluntly, but some of the opposition was gone from his voice. When you got as old at Buckshot, you noticed the little things. Like Jim Tennant's eyes. No longer *triste*, sad, as if the past had memories that persisted. The eyes had purpose now behind the grin as Jim holstered the six-shooter and reached for his hat.

"Clarkson'll have more chance than he ever gave anyone. Go get this Red Carney and tell him to ride out to the Ladrone with me tonight. Might as well keep crowding Clarkson's hand. I'll be at the livery barn getting a fresh horse."

V

Red Carney was openly sarcastic as he left the livery stable with Jim.

"I'm just fool enough to see what happens out at the Ladrone, mister."

"*Bueno*," Jim agreed.

"It ain't *bueno* to anyone but you," Red differed. "Damn it, I can't even handle your lingo, so's I can tell you how bad it is."

Long shadows were in the plaza just before sundown when they rode out of town. Buckshot Bledsoe came up from behind at a gallop and joined them.

"He hired me. Reckon I might as well tag along," the old man stated.

"That makes two of us crazy," retorted Red.

Jim spoke to Buckshot in Spanish. "Ride on back. We don't need you this trip."

"Your grandmother'll have whiskers before I do," Buckshot replied in the same language.

Red eyed them suspiciously. "What are you two palaverin' about?"

"He's tryin' to fire me."

"Maybe you're lucky."

"He hired me . . . an' I'm stayin' hired," Buckshot said stubbornly.

Red shrugged. "You're sure a hog for trouble . . . an' old enough to have better sense."

Jim said in Spanish. "Hear that? No sense. Better do like he says."

Buckshot ignored the advice, growling: "I never had no use fer a man who wouldn't belly up to his job after he took it on. I keep an eye on a feller I ain't sure'll do that."

Red grinned. "If I was suspicious, I'd say your eye was cut around on me."

"If the cinch fits you, buckle 'er on," Buckshot said grimly. "My eye is restless tonight. This young idjit is ridin' out to shake hands with the devil an' ain't got savvy enough to know what he's doin'. It's up to you an' me to ride herd on him."

Red grinned again. "You got the right idea. Tell Henry Clarkson you're lookin' out for him an' everything'll be all right."

Buckshot shifted to Spanish. "Just like I thought, Jim. He don't mean to help if he's needed. Likely he's planning to make a deal with Clarkson to help get you outta the way."

"Might be," conceded Jim.

"Send him back."

"I'd rather have him along to see what he's doing."

"What's the turkey talk about this time?" Red demanded.

"I give him advice an' he didn't have sense enough to take it," Buckshot said curtly. "The rest is your guess."

"I ain't guessin'. I'm just ridin' to see what happens," Red said with a shrug.

They reached Ladrone land as the silver moon disk was pushing up in the east. A wolf howled faintly and far to the west where the Ladrone peaks loomed blackly in the moonlight.

"Too bad Clarkson don't howl like that when he's huntin'," Buckshot growled.

"Gettin' spooky?" Red jeered as he swung down to open the wire gate.

"I'll holler when I am."

"Who's that at the gate?" a voice shouted off to the right.

Red dropped the gate and jumped to his horse and the rifle in the saddle scabbard as riders came galloping toward them and reined up inside the Ladrone wire, three men, bulking darkly in the moonlight, with rifles out and ready.

"We're ridin' to see Clarkson," Red said with a trace of dry humor. "And if Clarkson ain't at the house, we'll stay anyway. This feller owns part of the Ladrone now. He'll be givin' orders, too. You got any idea of stoppin' him?"

"Nope. Clarkson said he might be along. Didn't say nothin' about anyone else though. Ain't that you, Red Carney?"

Red was enjoying himself. "It ain't no one else, Jack Black. There's Red an' Black on the Ladrone payroll again. I'm back with you. The new boss has hired me. And Buckshot Bledsoe, too. You got anything to say about it?"

Jack Black was a bearded, massive man. His muttered oath as he quieted his horse showed how he felt. But he growled: "Ride on. That's Clarkson's business."

The guards stayed by the gate, silent, watchful in the moon-light.

When they were out of hearing, Red chuckled. "Clarkson holds all the cards but Jack Black ain't sure how they're bein' dealt. It like to gagged him to let me by."

"We ain't out here to take up any of your old feudin'," Buckshot said acidly.

"I ain't either," Red denied. "But keep that eye of your'n cut around for Jack Black. Dutch Walker ramrods the outfit and sees that the cattle's lined up. But Jack Black ramrods the gun hands. Them three rannies wasn't loafin' there by the gate for nothing. Bet there was more of them near if they was needed. Better tell your boss."

"No use tellin' him anything," Buckshot growled. "If he had any savvy, the three of us wouldn't be out here this way."

The Ladrone headquarters was on Manzanilla Creek, where old man Riggins had lived. Buildings had been added, low massive adobe buildings, each one as good as a fort in case of trouble. Corrals were well built and strong. Windmills were *creaking* briskly in the night wind and horses moved in the corrals as the three of them rode to the main house. From black shadows on the verandah a voice hailed them:

"Clarkson says for all of you to come in."

"They sent word from the gate we was coming. I don't like it," Buckshot muttered in Spanish.

In Spanish Jim said: "We'll see. Maybe he'll show some of his hand tonight. I'll do the talking. Keep our friend here quiet."

"What's he sayin'?" Red asked as they dismounted.

"Said for you an' me to mind our manners."

"I ain't got any manners." Red chuckled. "But I'm primed to see how Clarkson takes his new partner."

One man with a rifle guarded the verandah. Henry Clarkson bulked inside the lamplit doorway when Jim walked to it.

"Buenas noches, señor," Jim greeted him.

"Come in," Clarkson said.

All three carried their rifles in the house. The guns seemed out of place in the cool quiet under the log *vigas* of the big room where Clarkson took them.

Deer heads, a wildcat skin, a mountain lion skin were on the walls. Bearskins were on the floor. The furniture had been brought from the East and old Mexico.

Clarkson's fat pink face was smiling as he addressed Jim in

Spanish. "You like it?"

"Ah, *sí, señor.*"

"These are your men?"

"The ranch can use them, no?"

"We'll try." Clarkson nodded. "Anything on your mind to-night?"

"*Señor,* I but wanted to see this ranch of ours."

Henry Clarkson beamed. "All yours, *Don* Antonio. Have the goodness to be seated. You will have whiskey?"

"You trouble yourself too much, *señor.*"

Clarkson was smiling broadly as he motioned to a table against the wall that held a whiskey bottle and glasses. Red Carney read the gesture right and stepped to the bottle, grinning.

"First drink ever I got in here an' I'll make it a big one."

"That's right," Clarkson said. "Make it a big one, Carney. You'll need it."

"Yeah?" Red said, wheeling warily from the whiskey bottle. "Why'll I need it?"

Tension had been there in the room behind the smiling talk. Now suddenly the tension was out in the open, fairly crackling as Red hurled his terse question. Buckshot felt it, and Jim looked about the room for an answer.

Clarkson was still smiling but the broad fat face had gone pale with a new strain. The smile shaded to little more than a grimace before the threat on Red Carney's face.

Something moved slightly on the end wall of the room. Jim caught the movement. He looked at the other end of the room, then quickly glanced over his shoulder at the windows.

Clarkson saw him. The chuckle that followed had a rasp of unpleasant satisfaction.

"Tell him, *Don* Antonio, before he gets shot down like a dog," Henry Clarkson said in English. "And then we'll drink to Jim Tennant's luck in getting away from Zamora."

41

VI

Buckshot Bledsoe went for his six-gun. Jim was close enough to grab the wrist.

"Don't move, Buckshot! You too, Red! It's a trap! Look at the walls and windows!"

The harsh warning in English from the man who called himself *Don* Antonio Ponchito y Río stunned Red Carney for a moment. In that moment he looked and saw gun muzzles protruding from slits in the end walls and sighted through the open windows. Rifles. Six at least. Enough to drop all three of them before one could get a gun into action.

Red looked as if he were going for his gun anyway. Then he swore and lifted his hands shoulder high and spoke to Clarkson, and then to Jim.

"Might have knowed you'd have a trick, Clarkson. An' who'n hell are you, feller, makin' a fool outta me this way?"

"Jim Tennant's the name, Red. I bought into this ranch legal enough but I didn't figure Clarkson got news across the border so fast."

"Come and get them, Salazar!" Clarkson called.

"Salazar?" Jim repeated, frowning. "From Colonel Chavez's Hacienda Gorda?"

The man who entered the room with a drawn gun had the chunky build, heavy features, flat nose, thick lips, chocolate skin, and coarse black hair that showed a heavy mixture of Indian. Jack Black and another Ladrone gunman followed him in and helped disarm the prisoners.

Salazar's smile as he looked at Jim had gloating mockery in it.

"Plenty nice, thees *Don* Ponchito?" The blow of his hard hand split Jim's lip.

"Tally one," Jim said through his teeth. "An' I deserve it for letting you beg off that day on the Gorda."

Salazar hit him again. Henry Clarkson laughed as he poured whiskey in a glass and drank, smacking his lips.

"Too bad we can't watch Chavez handle you, Tennant. It'd almost be worth a ride to Zamora."

"So we're going back to Zamora?"

"In a day or two," Clarkson promised. "The sheriff here would hang you. But Chavez will do it better. From what Salazar tells me, I believe it. I've seen what Chavez can do. Salazar, get them out of here."

"Who's Chavez?" Red asked, as Jack Black's gun prodded him toward the door.

"He's the turkey that'll take you down to pin feathers an' then get the skin," jeered Black. "Red an' Black on the same payroll, is it? You're lucky. I'd have gut-shot you quick. This way you get a ride across the border."

Other gunmen appeared and helped escort the three prisoners back to a small, low outbuilding constructed of heavy peeled logs. The plank door was massive. The inside was a single dark room into which they were shoved. The door was slammed and padlocked on the outside.

Moonlight was visible through two small, barred openings under the ceiling. There were no windows. A match flared in the back corner as a voice greeted them.

"Make yourselves to home, boys. There's a bed for everyone . . . on the floor."

The face in the match light was like a dried, wind-scoured bit of the border desert from which keen eyes peered under bristling brows.

"Hondo!" Jim exclaimed.

"I sure rode hard to get my neck in a sling," Hondo said as the match went out. "Started soon as I got back to Zamora an' seen Seferino."

"Buckshot, Red . . . this is Hondo, who'll do anywhere," Jim

43

said. "I left word in Zamora for him and any friends to ride by the ranch here if they got a chance. Anyone come with you, Hondo?"

"I come alone," Hondo said, lighting another match. "Which one of you punched Chavez an' went out the window with Jim?"

"Wisht I'd bent a gun barrel on that sidewinder's head," Buckshot growled.

"You done worse," Hondo retorted. "The women are still laughin' at him behind his back. Chavez is frothin' and swearin' he'll get you both back."

Jim had been rolling a cigarette in the dark. He lighted it and his face was bleak in the match flare. His comment was bleak, too.

"Looks like he'll get us, too. I can't figure how he knew I'd be here. Seferino wouldn't talk. Or did he?"

"Not Seferino. You can trust that Mexican."

"But Salazar beat me here."

"When I hit Zamora," Hondo said, "Colonel Chavez sent for me and asked me personal what about this Ponchito who had been called a *gringo* name at the dance. Wouldn't believe me at first when I told him I had never heard the name Jim Tennant. Chavez didn't know where to find Jim Tennant then. He wanted to know. Right after that I seen Seferino an' left town in the night. Only Seferino knowed I was going. I made sure I wasn't followed an' I traveled fast. And south of the Laguna Tres Madres I run into nigh a dozen riders going north, too. Three of them were *gringo* hardcases. The rest was *vaqueros*. High man was Salazar who backed down when you called his bluff at the Gorda Ranch last year. Salazar knowed me right away and asked if I'd seen Ponchito. I told him not for a month. He told me what Chavez was going to do to Ponchito if he caught him. Just before Salazar left the ranch he heard about the trouble at the dance and had orders to keep an eye out for you, Jim. He knowed about the name Jim Tennant. But that's all he knowed. He didn't know I'd been to Zamora and talked with Chavez. He wasn't trailing you. He had other business. They were heading north and didn't want no company. Salazar made it plain after he got through askin' questions about you. So I cut off by myself. An' later I seen where they swung to the west after they passed the *laguna.*"

"Head that way from the Laguna Tres Madres," Buckshot said from the darkness, "and you'll come out at the Little Chipaderas. From there you can cut acrost the dry flats an' go north toward the Gila country."

"Or take Gray Ghost Cañon and reach the Ladrones," Jim amended. "When the 'breed herb doctor turned me loose, I went across the border that way. Salazar could have got his men here quicker that way."

"I ain't seen any of his men," Hondo said. "I got here yesterday and talked myself into a job at gun pay. Salazar rode in today, about half high sun before noon. Me bein' here didn't mean much to him after he heard I was workin' for the outfit. A man rode to town for the boss . . . and before sundown him and Salazar was makin' talk in the house. Orders come out to saddle and get ready for two or three days' work. I was saddling with the rest, and Salazar and this Clarkson, the boss, was watching, when Salazar grinned at me and told Clarkson to keep his eyes peeled for a friend of mine that the *gringos* called Jim Tennant and Colonel Chavez wanted in Zamora. Salazar said they knowed you acrost the border as Ponchito."

"So that's what happened?" Jim grunted. "Salazar told it right there."

"I wasn't sure," Hondo confessed. "Clarkson said he didn't know nothing about a man with those names and then remembered something in the house he'd forgot to show Salazar. They went in and I started figuring how to head you off. Next thing guns was in my back and I was in the house with Clarkson asking why I was here and who else'd come acrost the border with me. He was riled and jumpy."

"I'll bet he was," Jim said. "He thought Jim Tennant was long dead. I'd just told him in town my name was Ponchito and I owned part of this ranch now."

"I told him where to go," continued Hondo. "An' he had me throwed in here. What do you make of it, Jim?"

"It's bad," Jim said without hesitation. "I never thought Chavez, down there in Zamora, would get a hand in this business. I knew he'd been making big money in stolen cattle, even having it thieved from the folks in his district that he was supposed to protect, and trailed north across the border. And rustled stock on this side was run down to the ranches Chavez owns. But I didn't figure Chavez would have men riding this way so quick. And I didn't think they'd pay much attention to Buckshot calling me Jim Tennant at the dance. But that's Chavez. He's a fox."

"So now what?" Red Carney demanded out of the darkness.

"Hard to say about you, Red," Jim admitted. "It's Buckshot and Hondo and me. The sheriff here can put an old rustling charge against me if Clarkson says the word. But we'll get worse than that at Zamora. I've found bodies spread-eagled on cactus an' left for the sun and ants. Chavez is full of such tricks."

"I'll get it, too," Red told him dryly. "Mind telling me what's back of all this? I ain't heard enough yet to make sense."

"Hondo had better know, too," Jim said.

They listened to his terse outline of the past five years, and at the end Hondo's grim comment summed it up.

"Clarkson don't want anybody left to talk. He's on top and he aims to stay on top."

"The highest buzzard on the tree gets picked off first when the shooting starts," Jim pointed out. "And Henry Clarkson has roosted high an' fed on dead meat too long. Buckshot, how many folks around here would help themselves if they had a chance?"

Buckshot replied promptly. "Plenty . . . if they knowed there was somethin' they could do. But they'd have to be sure they had a chance to do it. Clarkson's gun riders have got 'em buffaloed. The best men have been kilt off or froze out or got disgusted an' moved on. Clarkson stays inside the law, an' he's got shut of folks most likely to make him trouble."

Two riders came to the small log building as Buckshot finished. One of the small barred air openings let in Henry Clarkson's jeering voice.

"*Adiós, Don* Antonio. Tomorrow or next day you start to Zamora. The first man who tries to break out gets shot. A pleasant trip south to all of you."

Red Carney replied with a savage and fluent stream of oaths. "Your number's up, Clarkson, if I get out with a gun!"

"Eees beeg noise from leetle rooster," Salazar jeered outside, and the two men rode away at a gallop.

Red swore again.

"That don't help," Jim said calmly. "Hondo, did those Clarkson riders leave?"

"Uhn-huh. Right after I was throwed in here."

"Know where they were going?"

"Nobody said."

"Salazar rode here alone?"

"I didn't see no one with him," Hondo grunted.

"Then they must be over around the Ladrones and Gray Ghost Cañon," Jim said. "Camping out. They don't want to be seen. Which means more crooked work. Can't be anything but rustling. Clarkson's gunmen are helping. They know the country. Clarkson's either got rustled beef on the ranch that he's ready to move or he knows where to gather a bunch for the

47

Chavez men to get over the border fast."

"Most likely both," Buckshot declared. "Nobody gits a chance to look over brands inside Clarkson's wire. What comes in stays in till Clarkson moves it ary way he likes. But there's good beef on the other ranches if a man knows where to look. Clarkson don't have to send honest meat across the border. It'll bring him more on this side. You can bet ary head that moves south is wet and crooked."

"That would settle Clarkson's hash before any honest jury if it was laid to him."

"It won't be," Buckshot stated dourly. "Clarkson'll git by with this like he has everything else. I ain't a man to say I told you so, Jim, but if we hadn't stuck our necks out by ridin' out here, we wouldn't be fixed like this."

"If we'd stayed in town, we wouldn't know all this," countered Jim.

"What good's it doin' us?"

"Maybe none. Anybody got a gun left?"

"They wasn't fool enough to miss no guns," Buckshot said glumly. "I got that knife that was stuck in my shoulder down in Zamora, though. Tied 'er down the back of my neck fer luck afore I rode after you an' Red. But a crowbar wouldn't get us through them logs, let alone a knife. An' they'll have plenty of guns ready to use when the door's opened."

Jim hammered on the door.

"Never mind that!" a gruff voice shouted outside.

"How about some water?"

"Won't be no water until Clarkson comes back with the key! Might be morning or later!"

"I figured there'd be a guard," Jim said under his breath. "Buckshot, gimme that knife . . . and start singing."

"Singin'?" Buckshot snorted. "I ain't that crazy. If cussin' would help, I'd try that."

Jim chuckled. "It'll have to be singing. These logs would stop an axe. But the *vigas* aren't too close together. There's only boards under the dirt. Clarkson's smart . . . but there's plenty ways to skin a cat. We'll skin him with this knife if there's enough noise so that the guard outside don't hear."

They saw instantly what he meant. The log walls and door were massive and strong. The roof had been built flat in the custom of the country. Cross-log vigas had been notched in atop the side walls. Rough-sawed boards had been laid over the vigas. Some two feet of dirt atop the boards formed the easily built adobe roof of the border country.

If a man could cut through the rough-sawed planks without the guard outside hearing, only dirt overhead would bar him from the sky. A knife, handled right, might cut through the tough, dry wood.

Hondo's husky whisper sharpened with hope. "It might work, Jim. Here's the box I was sittin' on."

Jim struck a match, held it up, selected a spot on the ceiling, and stepped on the box.

"I feel like a fool," Red Carney growled. "But I'd sing like a fool fer a chance at Clarkson. Come on, you birdies. Give 'em 'Mushmouth Magee'."

It wasn't music but it made noise. Jim grinned as Buckshot's harsh voice bayed out in the little low-ceilinged room, then grimly Jim attacked the boards above with the bone-handled knife.

It was hard, slow work, gouging, cutting across the wood grain overhead. Perspiration started to roll down Jim's face and neck. His arms began to ache. Bits of wood rained on his head and face.

When the third song ended, the guard outside called with loud sarcasm: "Sounds like coyotes yowlin' at the moon! Shut up an' go to asleep!"

"Come in and make us!" Red invited.

"I can hold out longer than you jaspers can howl without water."

Buckshot took a spell at the knife while Jim joined in the singing. Hondo and Red were too short to reach the ceiling boards from the low box.

When Buckshot gave out, Jim climbed back on the box. It took an hour and a half to get the first short length of board cut through against the supporting vigas and pulled down. Dirt showered down after it. Thereafter small showers of dry dusty dirt were constantly falling.

Buckshot got the second length of board out and staggered off the box, spitting dirt and growling as he brushed out his whiskers.

"Feels like digging with your face. We're a-gettin' there, boys . . . if they don't spot us. Two more boards an' we can git through."

Jim hacked and cut the third length of board out without stopping, and kept on desperately. The singing voices were harsh and cracked now as dry throats protested. The guard had cursed them and men had walked over from the bunkhouse to jeer, and then gone back to turn in.

Jim's arms were leaden with weariness as he wrenched the fourth board down and stumbled off the box.

"Hondo an' Buckshot can boost me up," he rasped. "Hondo can follow and pull Buckshot up. When you hear me outside, Red, jump for the box and let 'em pull you up."

"If they ain't waitin' on the roof when you poke your head out," Red warned.

"I'll know when I get up there. Let's go."

Red kicked on the heavy plank door and yelled for water as Hondo and Buckshot boosted Jim up into the small ceiling opening. The knife brought chunks of dry dirt down on the three of them. Jim's hand shoved through into the fresh air. Half a minute of furious work enlarged the hole. A boost shoved him through and up to a scrambling crouch on grass, weeds growing on the dirt.

Red was still kicking on the door when Jim reached the front of the roof. The guard below was cursing Red again and his voice broke in a choked yell as Jim's flying leap knocked him to the ground.

VII

But the knife wasn't needed. Knocked flat, breathless, the guard groped clumsily for his gun. Jim grabbed it from the holster and struck hard with the barrel.

Red had left the door as Jim jerked off the guard's gun belt and buckled it on. The choked yell apparently had not spread alarm for the other ranch buildings were dark, quiet, as Hondo followed by Buckshot and Red dropped off the low roof.

"Carry him to the corral and tie leather on some horses," Jim panted. "Our guns ought to be in the house. I'll look. If we have to scatter, get to the Merriman Ranch if you can. Buckshot, here's the knife. Don't let this *hombre* yell."

Red Carney growled a promise: "He won't."

It was almost midnight. Jim's shadow was plain in the bright moonlight as he skirted the house to the front porch.

No guard challenged. The front door was locked. Jim tried a front window. His guess was right. These front windows had been unlocked when they were trapped. Probably because the place was so well guarded no one had bothered to lock them. Jim was inside a moment later, gun out, listening.

He could detect no sign of life inside the house. Their gun belts and guns were on the table where Salazar and Jack Black had put them. Jim put them out the window and then, striking matches, investigated other rooms. Clarkson was not in the house.

A shout of alarm out back near the bunkhouse and a gunshot sent him plunging back to the front windows. Other shots were crashing in the night and horses were galloping around the house as Jim went through the window.

Hondo's yell broke around the corner of the house: "Jim! Jim!"

Scooping up belts and guns, Jim ran out into the moonlight as Hondo and the others reined up. Buckshot was riding bareback. Hondo was leading another horse, bridled but not saddled. He jerked out an explanation as Jim passed up the guns.

"One of them woke up afore we could get all saddled! We didn't have no guns."

Red Carney's yell of satisfaction split the night as he grabbed his guns and yanked his horse back to the side of the house. "I'll show them something now!"

Red vanished toward the back of the house. His handgun hammered out. Other guns blasted reply.

Jim mounted bareback and called: "Ride toward town! I'll get Red!"

But Hondo and Buckshot followed him. At the back corner of the house Red was yelling defiance and shooting from the saddle. Men had spilled out of the bunkhouse and now were shooting from the nearest cover. Lead was slapping into the house walls, screaming closely as Jim yanked his nervous horse to Red.

"You want to get shot up for nothing? Come on!"

Buckshot and Hondo opened up, and Red emptied his gun again before he reined around to leave.

"That'll give 'em something to think about," he declared with satisfaction.

"We've got plenty to think about ourselves! Are you staying in this?"

"Git some action stirred up an' watch me!" yelled Red.

"We'll scatter outside the Ladrone wire so they won't track us," Jim said crisply. "Meet again at the Hook 'n' Ladder." Jim rode beside Buckshot. "Here's your chance, old-timer. Every man who'll ride and fight is needed at the Hook 'n' Ladder quick. I want 'em all there by noon if possible. Tell 'em this is the chance to put Clarkson on the run. It's up to you to do this job. Hondo don't know them, an' Red wouldn't have much luck. Get help to spread the word . . . and they'll need plenty of guns and shells."

"Now you're talkin'!" Buckshot yelled. "I been a-waitin' fer this a long time! I'll git to Ben Kline's Bar T first! His men'll help spread the word!"

They found the Ladrone gate unguarded. "Clarkson's sent 'em out on his dirty work," Buckshot guessed.

They parted outside the wire.

Hondo started out with Jim, got directions, swung off by himself. Jim rode on alone, Indian style, planning what lay ahead if they were lucky.

Then as the moon dropped low, he reached Hook and Ladder grass. Bull Merriman's land. Lindy Lou's land, with Lindy Lou herself just ahead.

Dawn was pushing gray in the east when Jim looked from the last rise at Bull Merriman's big adobe house, outbuildings, windmills, and corrals down the slope.

The great grassy draw beyond fanned out into miles of rolling range. Nothing had changed. He himself might have been the old Jim Tennant, little more than a kid, riding with fast-beating heart for a word and laugh with Lindy Lou.

But when he rode closer, Jim discovered that there had indeed been changes. The Merriman place looked older, shabbier, run down. Money and work had been skimped lately; you could almost see Henry Clarkson's fat hand squeezing the life and strength out of the spread Bull Merriman had built.

Repeated knocks on the front door brought steps inside, and Lindy Lou's voice beyond the door. "Who is it?"

"Got to see you, lady. There's trouble."

The door opened and Lindy Lou stood there slim, straight, and sleepy-eyed in a belted robe and beaded buckskin slippers. The tall, *charro*-dressed figure, bareheaded, dirty, drew a gasp from her.

"I'm looking for a lady who used to know Jim Tennant," Jim said solemnly. "A sweet, pretty girl who used to meet him at the Black Rocks and ride with him. She had a dimple an' a freckle on her nose an' she used to. . . ."

"Jim!" Lindy Lou cried. "Jim Tennant! It . . . it is you!"

"Can I come in?"

Lindy Lou was laughing and crying. "They said you were dead, Jim. They . . . they buried you. For years I've put flowers on your grave. And in the bank yesterday you looked at me like a Mexican who couldn't speak English. Jim, is this a nightmare and you a ghost?"

"I'll bet a ghost can't do this." Jim chuckled, then kissed her.

A sharp command from behind them rasped with threat.

"Leggo her! I'll kill you for this!"

Old Rip Stevens had pulled on overalls and riding boots and run from the bunkhouse with a rifle. Now he was ready to shoot as two more men rounded the house at a run with guns.

Lindy Lou was laughing and turning red. "Wait, Rip! This is Jim Tennant! It . . . it's all right!"

"Who?" Rip almost yelled. He straightened, blinking, peering, and spoke wildly to the other two from the bunkhouse. "She says that's Jim Tennant who grabbed an' kissed her! Am I a-seein' right an' a-hearin' right?"

Fogey Wilson was another oldster. Dan Coleman was middle-aged. Both had been on the Hook and Ladder, too, in the old days. Fogey Wilson eyed the two in the doorway and said dryly: "Don't see the lady balkin' or kickin' in the traces. Must be Jim, if you could get behind that dirty face an' them fancy clothes."

Jim looked ruefully at his hands and touched his face. "I forgot the dirt, boys. We cut through an adobe roof over at the Ladrone Ranch. Soon as you can dress and saddle, there's some riding to do quick, if Lindy Lou says the word."

"Whatever you think, Jim," Lindy Lou said, her eyes still full of wonder. "I'll dress and start breakfast while you wash and the others get ready. You can tell us about it."

When they were all together in the big kitchen, Jim talked fast, summing up the happenings of five years ago tersely.

"Fire was falling on my face when I woke up in that Antelope Cañon barn. Wasn't a chance to fight and get away. You remember there was an iron water tank over in a corner of the barn, with water for the horses when the cañon went dry."

"We hauled that old tank to a windmill two years ago." Fogey Wilson nodded.

"Well, I crawled in and stayed under water between breaths while the barn burned down around me," Jim said. "It nearly boiled me anyway. The men outside were sure nobody was alive an' rode away till the fire cooled off, and, while they were gone, I crawled out and got away. And kept going." When he finished telling of the escape from the Ladrone Ranch, Jim said: "It's time to stop Henry Clarkson. I own part of the Ladrone now, but I need help. Get men here you can trust. I'll do the talking. It won't be hard to get them interested. There'll be plenty of local brands on the cattle that Clarkson is starting over the border."

"I'll bet," old Rip Stevens growled. "Folks get no help from Lan Hanson, the sheriff. Miss Lindy Lou, you gonna back Jim up in this?"

"Of course I am, Rip. I've been wanting something like this to happen . . . and I couldn't do it myself. Jim will."

"Jim'll make everything all right now," Dan Coleman drawled innocently.

"Of course he will." Then Lindy Lou blushed as Dan burst out laughing and old Rip and Fogey Wilson chuckled.

"You three laughing hyenas have got more to do than joshing Lindy Lou," Jim warned with a sheepish grin.

"Can't help it after watchin' her lookin' at you." Dan chuckled. "You come back to life an' brought her back to life, too. Things is different already. We'll scratch dirt an' make the dust fly now. Soon as we finish this grub, we'll hightail."

The three of them galloped off in high spirits a few minutes later. A while later Red Carney, and then Hondo arrived. Lindy Lou gave them breakfast.

"We'd better get out to the bunkhouse and catch a nap," Jim decided. "Lindy Lou can shake us out if any of Clarkson's men show up."

It was past noon when Dongie Taylor, of the small Rafter B Ranch, shouted them out and gave Jim a mighty handshake as he rolled off the bunk.

VIII

"You're a sight for eyes, Jim," he said heartily. "Come out and make talk! There's a bunch been waitin' for you to wake up and more coming."

Dongie Taylor had been a friend in the old days. Besides him, better than a dozen men had already ridden in. Some Jim had known. Some were strangers. None of them looked prosperous.

Hard work and worry marked most of them. But they had brought guns and a show of hopeful spirit as Jim shook hands and answered questions that were fired at him.

Another two hours doubled their number. Horses had been watered, fed, and rested. Guns were looked to. Lindy Lou was kept busy feeding each new arrival.

Jim was smiling when he stepped into the hot kitchen where Lindy Lou was still working.

"It's better than I hoped. They're ready to ride and fight."

"You've given them hope again," Lindy Lou told him. "You own part of the Ladrone Ranch now . . . and you're ready to fight on their side. The law's on their side and they see what they can do if they get together and follow you. Oh, Jim, we can't fail now. This is the last chance."

"I know," Jim agreed soberly. "And we won't fail."

"Jim . . . if anything happens to you. . . ." Lindy Lou's voice caught. "I thought you were dead once. I . . . I couldn't stand it again."

Flour smudged the cheek Jim tipped up to kiss. He was smiling.

"When we leave, you start watching. I'll be back . . . to stay."

"Jim, the sheriff's coming with some men!" a shout outside warned.

Four riders were nearing the men out by the bunkhouse and corrals when Jim joined them.

"He's got Coly Johnson, his deputy, an' them two men from the Ladrone he keeps deputized," one of the men declared uneasily. "Likely there's a bunch of Ladrone men somewhere close."

"I'll do the talking," Jim said. "Back me up is all I ask, boys."

Lan Hanson, the sheriff, was a new man on the range, a big man, beardless, weathered, with a steel-trap mouth and two six-guns. Coly Johnson, Hanson's deputy, was lanky, raw-boned, with a loose smile that might have meant anything as he reined up beside the sheriff. The other two men looked as hard as Jack Black, leader of the Ladrone gunmen.

"Howdy, men. Something going on here?" Hanson asked civilly enough as he looked around the gathered crowd.

Jim saw the two gunmen go tense and exchange satisfied glances as he stepped forward. They knew the *charro* suit and were looking for him.

"We're glad to see you, Sheriff," Jim said. "This is a posse ready to look for rustlers. You can swear them in and they'll be ready to help you."

Hanson's face hardened. "I'll call my own posse together when I need it. Who are you?"

"I'm Jim Tennant, part owner of the Ladrone Ranch. We'll know each other better before long. Right now it's rustlers we're looking for . . . and you're the man to lead us."

The sheriff nodded. "Rustlers is right. I've got a warrant. . . ."

"Wait a minute, Sheriff!" Jim broke in. "Hondo, Red?"

"We got 'em covered, Jim!" Hondo answered over to the right. And Red Carney's voice on the left was cold and vicious: "I'll gut-shoot Shorty Thomas soon as that son-of-a-bitch touches his gun! An' I'll get that deputy the next shot!"

Shorty Thomas, Jim surmised, would be the Ladrone gunman whose tense arm moved hastily away from his body when he heard Red.

"What is this?" the sheriff exploded angrily. "Are all you men going against the law?"

Jim chuckled. "We're helping the law. Throw down your guns, and that warrant, too. And then get ready to deputize and lead us. You're the law and we're back of you, Hanson."

"I'll. . . ."

"No, you won't," Jim cut in again. "We're the ones that are

backing you today, not Henry Clarkson. Shuck the guns and deputize us."

"Are you men with this law dodger?" Lan Hanson demanded, glaring at the ranchers.

"They're with the law and waiting to be deputized," Jim said. "I'm the one who's telling you to do it quick."

"No, you ain't, Jim!" Dongie Taylor yelled. "We're all saying so, too! If it's law dodgers Hanson wants, we'll help him find them!"

"You bet we're with you, Tennant!" Dongie was supported. And a third man shouted: "We'll all of us make sure they don't try no tricks! We know who gives Lan Hanson orders!"

Glowering before the threatening crowd, Hanson surrendered his guns, handed down a folded warrant calling for the arrest of Jim Tennant, and surlily deputized them all.

"You men'll be sorry for this," he promised angrily.

"For years we've been sorrier over other things," Dongie Taylor retorted. "Jim, we're ready to cut Ladrone cattle an' read brands."

Hanson and his men were put in the lead where they could be watched. The ranchers, twenty-three strong, were laughing, talking, exuberant as they swept down the wide grassy draw and headed toward Ladrone land. Lindy Lou had been right. These men had new life, new hope. They were believing Jim Tennant, backing him, looking for him to catch Henry Clarkson outside the law.

Jim rode beside Dongie Taylor and repeated his plans.

"Clarkson sent men west toward Ladrone Mountain. We'll find them over that way helping those *vaqueros*. And we'll find plenty of cattle that don't belong on Ladrone land. It may take gun play to cut them out and make sure. But we'll do it if these men don't back out."

"They won't," Dongie promised. "Look at them."

Jim looked around, and nodded with satisfaction.

Two hours hard riding brought them to the Ladrone line fence and an armed rider who came galloping to the wire with a shouted warning: "Nobody's allowed inside this fence!"

"This is a sheriff's posse!" Jim called. "Ride back and tell Clarkson we're coming! Tell him Jim Tennant's with the sheriff!"

The man wheeled his horse and spurred into a gallop toward the west.

Jim chuckled as one of the men cut wire to let them through. "I didn't know whether he'd do it or not. Hanson, that's where I thought we'd find him. Over toward Ladrone Mountain. You ready to make arrests?"

Hanson was still ugly. "I'll make arrests," he said darkly, "and it won't be rustlers. Clarkson don't stand for rustlers on his land. And the law and the folks who elected me won't stand for this."

Some of the men looked uneasy when they heard that. Jim gave them something else to think about. "That man'll get out of sight," he warned.

The Ladrone man had left at a full gallop and kept going. Jim called off the pursuit in less than a mile.

"We'll run our horses out. He's making a beeline for the Gray Ghost Cañon trail. We'll find what we're after."

A little later one of the men called: "That feller's slowed down! See him walkin' his horse on that second rise?"

Jim frowned when he saw that the man was right. Hondo rode over and spoke from a mouth corner: "Funny that feller slowed down when he did. Wouldn't be wantin' us to foller him, would he?"

"That just struck me," Jim admitted.

A little later a man pointed ahead and called: "Ain't that trail dust to the left of that shoulder of the mountain?"

Most of them could see the faint drifting haze low down against Ladrone Mountain. Only a sizable beef or horse herd trailing on dry ground would lift such a steady haze of dust. The Ladrone guard was still heading toward the spot.

Spirits lifted once more and the men rode faster. But the sun was already sliding down on Ladrone Mountain and the dust was far ahead. Then the sun was gone and purple shadows were preceding twilight when they reached the strung-out trail herd of several hundred head.

Two Mexican *vaqueros* in high-peaked straw sombreros riding drag stared impassively as the armed riders galloped past. The chunky dark-faced man who came spurring back with two more *vaqueros* was Salazar. He stared malignantly at Jim Tennant.

"Get these cattle ready for a cut!" Jim ordered curtly.

"What ees?" Salazar protested as he was surrounded. "Thees cattle we buy from Ladrone Ranch."

"Where's Clarkson?"

"*¿Quién sabe?*" Salazar shrugged. "*Señor* Clarkson take money to hees bank, I theenk. *Si.* Hees bank. You wan' bill of sale for thees cattle?"

"Never mind a bill of sale! Get 'em ready for a cut!"

"I don't like this, Jim," Hondo said in a low voice. "Ain't one of Clarkson's men here. The brands I've seen so far look all right."

Jim nodded glumly. "Looks like Clarkson's pulled a trick. We'll cut 'em and make sure."

Disappointment grew on expectant faces as the herd was bunched and inspected in the fading light. Here was no fight, no rustlers, no crooked work to pin on the Ladrone outfit. Here was a small trail herd branded right, sold legally, and heading peacefully south. Lan Hanson was sneering with satisfaction when the cut was over.

"Rustlers, huh? I warned you men that Tennant was talking

you into trouble. Help me arrest him like you should have in the first place and I'll see what I can do about clearing the rest of you."

"Jim, this is the devil," Dongie Taylor said frankly. "The men were sure you were right . . . and now look where we are. 'Most dark now . . . and we're away out here like a bunch of lost sheep." He was saying mildly what many of the men were thinking.

"You men know Clarkson!" Jim told them. "You can see this is a trick. When Clarkson heard we got away last night, he figured there might be trouble . . . and got ready for it. The Ladrone bunch is out on the range here somewhere."

"How do we know where they are?" old John Posten demanded heavily. "Clarkson outsmarted you, Tennant, like he's outsmarted everyone else. We've got our ranches and our families to think about. We listened to you and you were wrong. Most likely you'll be wrong on anything else. We tried to help you when we thought you were right. Now we look like a bunch of fools. We don't doubt you meant well, but I don't want to get any deeper, the way this has turned out."

"I know how you feel," Jim said, "but you and the other men have still got your chance. These Mexicans didn't ride across the border to buy legal cattle. They can buy cheaper where they came from. I know that country. The fact that they're here is all the sign you need on Clarkson. Stay with me tonight and maybe tomorrow and we'll find what they came north to get. It'll be beef that no bill of sale will cover."

"What's your idea, Jim?" Dongie Taylor said hopefully.

Lan Hanson's harsh voice warned them before Jim could answer. "I'm giving you men your chance with the law now. Back me up in serving that warrant on Tennant and I'll see that the rest of this is forgot. If there's any crooked work going on,

I'll see about that, too. I'm the sheriff and the law will take care of it."

At Jim's side, Hondo whispered: "He's gettin' 'em, Jim. Think of somethin' fast or we'll have to fight back to the border."

"We'll have to hunt Clarkson and they don't want to hunt," Jim said heavily. "Who's that coming?"

It was too dark now to see far but the drumming hoofs of a galloping horse on the back trail could be clearly heard.

"I hope it's Clarkson," Hondo gritted, reining around to meet the approaching rider.

But it was not Clarkson, or any of his riders. It was Lindy Lou, riding a lathered horse. Jim spurred to meet her.

"Jim! Did you find Clarkson? Is it all right?"

"No. Clarkson tricked us."

"I was afraid so!" Lindy Lou cried. "I've been trailing you and trying to catch you. Jim, Buckshot Bledsoe is dead. He rode back to the Ladrone Ranch to look around and was shot. But he stayed on the horse and reached my house. He was dying, Jim. He was out of his head. But he kept mumbling . . . 'Tell Jim, Paso Diablo . . . tell Jim, Paso Diablo!'"

"Good girl! Don't tell anyone!" Jim called to the men who were gathering around them: "Clarkson's men killed Buckshot Bledsoe. But Buckshot sent word where to go. We're all right now . . . and Clarkson won't be looking for us. That's good enough, isn't it?"

"Good enough for me!" Dongie Taylor yelled. "If Miss Merriman can bring word clear out here, I can ride on to find Clarkson now."

Lindy Lou's ride, the sight of her far out here by Ladrone Mountain, shamed more than one man who was wavering. Shouts of agreement backed up Dongie. In short minutes they were riding again, Lindy Lou with them on a fresher horse that one of Hanson's gun deputies had been riding. Jim had tried to make her go home but her logic had been unanswerable.

"I can't go back alone, Jim, and none of the men can be spared to go with me. I'll ride with you and . . . and shame anyone who wants to hang back."

"And get hurt . . . maybe shot?"

"If trouble starts, I'll get out of the way, Jim. I'll not make any trouble. But this is my business, too. Father would have been here in my place. And I want to be near you. I . . . . I want to be sure you'll come back this time."

And after that there was no more time to talk.

IX

Paso Diablo—Devil Pass—was past the *malpais* belt south of the Ladrone range. Lava flows, rocky ridges, and pinnacles were cut by deep-scoured arroyos—fifteen miles of *malpais* ending in Devil's Ridge, a black, frowning barrier to the way south.

Paso Diablo knifed through the ridge between sheer walls of rock. In spots half a dozen riders could not move abreast. The *malpais* belt was dry. There was no water for thirty miles south of the pass. And now in the midnight moonlight the water-scoured sand at the entrance to Paso Diablo was white and smooth. Lan Hanson's accusing anger rasped from a dry throat.

"No cattle have been through here! Tennant's made fools of you again! Maybe you'll see it this time!"

Hours back men and horses had watered at a Ladrone windmill tank beyond the *malpais*. Now they were dry and that far windmill was the nearest water. Horses were dead beat, men tired, tempers on a hair trigger. Jim sensed what was coming in the sullen silence that followed Hanson's words.

"Clarkson's men couldn't have started to drive this way until late, and it's hard trailing across the *malpais*," Jim told them. "We cut across from Ladrone Mountain and made fast time. I figured to beat them here. Buckshot Bledsoe knew what he was talking about."

"Maybe he did . . . an' maybe he didn't!" old John Posten snapped. "But I've had enough. Don't know whether I can get my hoss back to water now. You don't know what you're doin', Tennant. I'm quittin' you. There's the pass to the border. Better take it quick before Hanson starts you back to San Angelo jail."

"That the way the rest of you feel?" Jim asked.

Lindy Lou, siding her horse close to him, cried out at their silence: "You can't do it! Henry Clarkson will own you body and soul if you quit Jim now! Can't you see this is your last chance? My father would have known Jim was right! He would have done what Jim is doing! He wouldn't have been afraid!"

"We ain't afraid," John Posten said stubbornly. "We've just had enough truck with Tennant's ideas. He better cut and run before the sheriff takes him in."

"You men are deputies," Lan Hanson reminded. "Give me my guns and help arrest Tennant and his friends, dead or alive. They'll get a fair trial."

"They're gonna do it, Jim," Hondo warned under his breath.

"You and Red ride south," Jim said through tight lips. "Stay here with them, Lindy Lou. I've got an idea. Maybe it'll work."

Before the others knew what he was doing, he rode hard out into the moonlight. Lan Hanson's shout rang after him: "Stop them! Shoot them! Ride after them!"

But no guns were fired. Riders followed. Two riders. Hondo and Red Carney, following Jim into the *malpais,* back toward the Ladrone range.

"They're makin' a show of coming after us!" Hondo called as he caught up.

"I figured some of them would!" Jim yelled back. "They've got to head back for water anyway. But they're not shooting. They're not ready for that. Why didn't you two head south?

Nobody would have followed you into the pass."

"We're fools like you," Hondo retorted gruffly. "There ain't much run left in these horses, Jim."

"I know, but they'll have to do what they can."

Two miles—three miles—the *malpais* was stark and torturous under the moon. White sandy arroyo beds were like bleached, sinuous bones over which water roiled during infrequent storms.

They rounded a turn in one wide arroyo—and saw a dark moving mass ahead that might have been a shoulder-high wall of water coming majestically toward them. But the sound through the night was the uneasy bawl of hurrying cattle.

"There they are!" Jim called, lifting his rifle. "I thought we'd meet 'em somewhere out here if Buckshot was right! Hell's gonna bust loose in a minute!"

"Let 'er bust!" Red yelled back. "This is what I've been taggin' along to see!"

Three riders ahead of the cattle spurred toward them. The leader hailed them. "Who's that?"

"Come an' see, Jack Black!" Red Carney yelled. "And come shootin'!"

Black's gun flash was visible before the report and the high-pitched sound of the passing bullet.

"Get 'em before the swing men ride up!" Jim shouted. "Scatter those steers! Stampede!"

Red Carney's rifle shot cut off his words. The rider just behind Jack Black pitched to the arroyo sand.

"Tally one!" Red whooped, spurring forward. "Jack Black's my man!"

Hondo uttered an Indian yell as he followed Jim toward the blazing guns of Jack Black and the other man.

The first steers had stopped uneasily. Those behind jammed up in a bawling mass. Then suddenly the mass broke up the steep sides of the arroyo and ahead in the first run of a panic-stricken stampede.

The two Ladrone men jerked their horses around but they were too late to do anything. Big steers were charging at them in a blind run. They abandoned the gunfight and drove their horses up the arroyo bank out of the way. Red swerved up the same side of the arroyo after them, and Jim and Hondo followed.

The moonlight was bright enough to see clearly the man who had plunged to the arroyo sand, who was suddenly lying there alone as his horse bolted, who struggled weakly on hands and knees—and then went down under the stampeding steers.

Jim swallowed and felt a little sick. And there was no time to think more of it. The earth seemed to be shaking, even to men in the saddle, as the big steers erupted wildly out of the arroyo and scattered into the badlands night.

Swing and drag riders of the herd were visible, too, in the moonlight, riding wildly for safety, helpless for the moment to do anything but scatter out.

"Red!" Jim shouted.

But Red Carney was recklessly following Jack Black and another. The two Ladrone men vanished in a depression. Red followed them, his six-gun blasting shots.

A few moments later Jim's horse plunged down the steep rocky slope and Red's horse was kicking in a heap at the bottom. The stocky man's body was crumpled at one side among the rocks.

The Ladrone riders had stopped on the opposite slope and were shooting back as running steers plunged by over to Jim's left.

Jim's six-gun was empty. His rifle magazine was full. He dismounted beyond Red and had the rifle up almost as soon as he hit the ground.

Ricocheting lead screamed off a rock by Jim's leg and the

Ladrone men wheeled to ride over the crest of the slope out of sight. Jack Black's bearded face had been clear enough in the moonlight—and the bulk of the other man could be no one but Henry Clarkson.

Black was a dark mass in the rifle sights as Jim squeezed the trigger. The snapping report knocked the Ladrone man out of the saddle as if he had been axed. A second later Hondo's horse came tearing down the slope to a rearing stop.

"Jim, them Ladrone men are bunching up and heading this way! They can see now we're alone!"

"That's Henry Clarkson riding back toward them," Jim said. "Jack Black won't be helping any more. That was him I knocked out of the saddle. Wait'll I look at Red."

The stocky gunman was dead. His face sober, Jim climbed back in the saddle.

"He was good enough in his way," he said quietly. "And he'd feel better because I got Jack Black."

"What about them Ladrone men?"

"We can't handle the bunch alone. Make a ride for it."

The mad stampede was scattering far over the badlands. By daybreak most of the cattle would be back toward water and grass, back on Henry Clarkson's land with all the damning evidence of their brands.

Jim led the way out of the depression and with the moonlight lighting them they were sighted. A yell of discovery rang out. Snapping gun reports marked ten or a dozen riders converging after them.

"These hosses can't run far!" yelled Hondo.

"They won't have to!" Jim called back.

Even fresh horses would not have lasted long through that broken, torturous country. But the Ladrone men gained fast, shooting as they rode. Bullets screamed, whined uncomfortably close. The end was only a matter of time for the pursuit to draw closer.

Hondo called: "They'll get us, Jim! These horses won't last!"

"Keep going!" Jim retorted—and his words met a burst of yells off to the right as a line of riders burst over a low ridge. "A gunfight was all those ranchers needed!" he yelled to Hondo, wheeling back.

The Ladrone men had bunched to a stop. A bullet from Jim's rifle drove one horse down, floundering. Blasting rancher guns sent a second wounded horse bolting with its rider. The Ladrone men fired a few scattered shots and broke back to the north. The dismounted rider staggered to his feet and limped after them, waving, calling frantically.

Hondo rode toward the man while Jim swerved to meet the ranchers.

"Stay together, men!" he shouted. "Let 'em go! They're licked!"

But it was half a mile farther on before the last of the strung-out ranchers turned back. Jim led them to the spot where Red Carney sprawled among the rocks. On the opposite slope Jack Black lay alive and sullen where Jim had shot him out of the saddle.

"So Clarkson wasn't smart enough to keep outta trouble after all," Black gasped when Jim stood by him. "I knew we'd better get you an' that Red Carney before we bothered with the cattle. I got Red anyway, damn him."

"And it'll be the last gun work you do," one of the ranchers told him. "From now on there'll be law in these parts that works. Here, Hanson! Put him under arrest!"

Black pushed himself up to a sitting position. His sullen voice grated. "Is that Lan Hanson with you men?"

Lan Hanson had changed. He was gruff and positive.

"It ain't no one else. You'll go back under arrest, Black. We'll get to the bottom of this."

"You double-crossin' skunk. You must've led 'em to us." Jack Black had his gun out and roaring before anyone could stop him.

Lan Hanson fell, the third bullet smashing into his body before Jim could plunge in and wrench the gun away from Black.

"Should've knowed he'd do us dirt sometime. But he won't double-cross no one else," Black gasped as he collapsed on the stony ground.

"He holed Hanson smack in the face. Kilt him clean," announced the rancher who was first to the sheriff's side.

A shout several hundred yards away drew attention. It was Hondo calling: "Any more trouble?"

And it was Hondo who came riding slowly and driving a heavy-set, limping figure ahead of him.

"Got the old bull skunk hisself," Hondo announced. "Wasn't no trouble to make him talk. He's guilty as all get out. Here he is."

A rancher shouted: "Git him to a tree and string him up!" Other men vociferously approved the suggestion.

"You can't do that, men," Jim told them. "You wanted honest law. You rode out today to get honest law. You got what you wanted. Now let honest law handle Clarkson."

"Tennant's right," old John Posten lifted his voice. "If we needed the law when we were down, we'll need it worse when we're on top. I got an idea." Posten was still gruff as he turned to Jim. "I guess most of us are ready to eat crow. We thought you'd made fools outta us, Jim, and we acted like fools. We needed you and we'll keep needing you. Hanson swore you in as a deputy, so there ain't nothing to stop you from taking Clarkson back to jail. We'll back you up. And we'll see you voted in as sheriff. That's what we want. How about it?"

Lindy Lou had ridden up in the background. Now, coming

forward, she was unabashed, although the eyes of all the men were on her.

"Jim's been away a long time," she said. "He came back to settle down. He wanted to keep away from trouble. Isn't that what you told me, Jim? Don't you want to stay at home from now on?"

Jim stepped over and took her hand. It was icy and trembling from the strain of the past hour. If the men who were looking at them, the friends, the old neighbors and the strangers there, were reading their two minds, it did not matter. They could all see Jim's grin in the moonlight.

"I've got a ranch," Jim told them, "and I'll be getting married. I'm home to stay . . . and I aim to stay at home."

★ ★ ★ ★ ★

LODEVILLE

★ ★ ★ ★ ★

The year 1937 began with a major work, "Murder Caravan," a six-part serial that was sold to *Detective Fiction Weekly*. This was followed by three short novels, two of them Westerns. The fourth short novel that year was also a Western, titled "Lodeville Calls a Gun Doctor," completed in May. It was published in *Star Western* under this title in the issue dated August, 1937. For its first appearance in book form the title has been abbreviated.

I

Pop Marcy owned the Gunsight Mine outside Lodeville, and the Gunsight Bar in Lodeville. And tonight Pop Marcy was curtly positive in telling the tall, sullen young man fronting the Gunsight bar that he'd had enough. "You'll get no more booze here tonight, Halliday," Pop said.

Five men lined the bar. A four-handed stud game filled one of the tables. Men hugged the roaring stove at the back. A moment after Pop Marcy spoke, two men dived through the front door, stamping snow off their feet, brushing it from their coats, and swearing at the blizzard.

The norther had struck hard at dusk. Sleet had turned to fine hard snow that swirled and drifted on the icy ground, blotting out the lights of the mines beyond town.

In the Gunsight Bar, Halliday pushed a flat-brimmed hat back off his moist forehead. His sheepskin jacket covered a gaudy woolen shirt; his stained corduroy trousers were tucked inside high-laced boots caked with drying mud. He spoke truculently: "Trying to start another argument . . . by making out I'm drunk, eh?"

Pop Marcy's white eyebrows, mustache, and white hair had an alert, bristling look. His gray eyes were cold as he swabbed a damp rag over the bar top.

"You've had enough, I said, Halliday."

"I'm sober enough to make you another offer for your damned mine!"

"You'll never be sober enough to buy it. An' there's a heap more room for you over at the Thirty-Deep Bar. We're crowded in here."

A thick-chested man beside Halliday laughed. "That oughta hold you, Nelse. Ike, gimme the bottle again. That wind hangs icicles on my liver."

Ike, the lanky night bartender, put the bar bottle out. Nelse Halliday leaned over and caught it. "I'll take mine now, Jerry. Your drink's on me."

Pop Marcy snatched up a bung starter and smashed the bottle. Swearing, Nelse Halliday jumped back from the cascading whiskey.

"You stiff-necked old hellion! I ought to rub your face in that!"

Pop Marcy vaulted over the bar, brandishing the bung starter. "Get going, damn you!"

Halliday wiped stinging liquor from an eye and reached inside his coat. "I'll gun whip some sense in you."

Big Jerry drew his gun. Two other guns across the room came out. "Don't hit him, Nelse," Big Jerry warned.

Nelse Halliday looked at the gun. Then he shoved his revolver back and started outside. He lurched slightly as he turned at the front door, scowling.

"Marcy, you're asking for trouble. You'll get it. Remember, don't come to me when you need help."

The door behind Halliday flew open. A snow-whitened figure staggered in against him. Nelse Halliday turned with an oath.

The stranger was a head shorter than Halliday, and seemed thin and gaunt inside his old leather chaps and a sheepskin coat. His head was bare; snow had driven inside the coat collar and caked in his hair. His face was blank with surprise as Halliday turned on him, swung a hard fist, and knocked him down.

The stranger's right arm had been tucked stiffly under his

coat. As he hit the floor, the arm flopped out helplessly. The stranger's groan was so filled with agony that even Halliday's angry oath died uneasily.

Slowly, white with pain, the stranger came to a knee, and then to his feet. Breath whistled through his clenched teeth. He was grinning, and his face was livid and threatening despite the grin.

"So you're the kind who does that. I'll remember you, mister." He moved unsteadily toward the bar.

Halliday slammed the door as he went out, but he caught the first part of Pop Marcy's blast of anger.

"My God, the feller's arm is busted, an' Nelse knocked him down! Git a chair, somebody . . . Ike, some likker. Somebody run for Doc Cloud. Where's some snow? His face is froze."

There was no lack of help to put a chair under the stranger, to pour a drink in him, to start the frost out of his face with handfuls of snow.

Doc Cloud, bulky as a bear in a moth-eaten bearskin coat and fur cap, came stamping in with his bag. He shed his bearskin coat, looking almost as huge without it. His moon-like face was jovial as he waved the men back.

"Give him room, boys. Let's have a look at this arm."

Doc Cloud was surprisingly quick and gentle as he got the sheepskin coat off. Skillfully he cut the woolen shirt sleeve and the heavy underwear beneath. He examined the arm, and pursed his thick lips in a soft whistle.

"Wrap him up and get him over to my office," he ordered, reaching for the bearskin coat. "Bring a quart, Pop. If he don't need it, I will."

Pop grumbled: "You'll need it anyway, Doc. Your last quart was 'way back almost at noon. I been looking for you for over an hour."

They carried the stranger down the street to Doc Cloud's office, speaking of Nelse Halliday as they went.

"Halliday slunk out like a skunk runnin' from his stink," said Pete Elden of the J Bar U disgustedly. "That's what comes of havin' an uncle leave a fortune to a swelled head."

"Old Nelse wasn't much better," Big Jerry grunted. "He tried to hog everything in sight an' run over anybody that got in his way."

"Old Nelse run over 'em to their faces, fair an' square . . . an', when he swallered a pint of whiskey, he was still a man." Pete Elden chuckled with anticipation. "Did you see that stranger's face when he come up from the floor? If I don't miss my guess, Nelse Halliday's in for trouble when the stranger's arm gets well."

The odor of chloroform was heavy in the little back office as Doc Cloud coughed and lowered the whiskey bottle. "There he is," said Doc, nodding at the operating table. "Now what, Pop? Where's he going to stay?"

They were alone with the patient. Several of the men who had come with them were loitering in the front room. Pop squinted at the motionless figure on the table. "Can't move him till he wakes up, can we, Doc?"

"He oughtn't to get out in the cold after having chloroform."

"There was only sixty-five cents we found on him. Even his gun was gone."

Pop stepped to the table and opened the shirt. A fresh bandage had been put around the stranger's middle.

"I locked the door," said Doc Cloud, "an' fixed him while you went back to the saloon. It's a bullet wound, Pop. Not so old, either. Rib busted, and a lot of meat gouged out. It hasn't had much chance to heal."

Pop closed the shirt and hesitated. "He ain't a bad-lookin' young fellow."

"Can't always tell. Some mighty tough *hombres* look like yearlings . . . when they ain't ridin' on moonless nights."

"He won't get any kind of break over at the hotel without money. I'll take him home."

"I was waitin' for that," grumbled Doc Cloud. "But if a sheriff comes lookin' for a man with a bullet wound in his side, this gent will have to be given up."

"I'll get a wagon, a pile of blankets, an' a tarp to move him," said Pop, turning to the door. "An' you don't need to wag your tongue about it until the sheriff shows up, you over-sized old rum-pot."

"When a cantankerous old wolf can tell me what to do, I'll start drinkin' water," retorted Doc Cloud. "Leave me out another bottle before you close up. It's going to be a long night an' a cold one . . . and the devil only knows what'll be knocking at the door in the morning."

In the morning, when the stranger opened his eyes, a girl was standing at the foot of the bed. He was sick and weak; the pine walls of the room seemed to wobble for a moment.

He saw her clearly. She was pink-cheeked, brisk, small, and pretty as something out of a dream. Blonde hair swirled above her forehead, her eyes had laughter shadows, and her nose tilted up the pertest bit. She caught his widening stare and chuckled slightly. "How do you feel this morning, Shorty Burgess?"

His face was drawn, haggard under the stubble. And, too, it was hard, Kathleen Allen thought—too hard for a man so young. But his slow grin wiped away much of the hardness.

"So you know my name?" he said. "Who are you?"

"Kathleen Allen."

Caution, cold and wary, edged his look for an instant. Then it left, as if he had put it away with a hasty effort. "Where am I?"

"This is Pop Marcy's house. He owns the saloon."

"Yeah . . . I remember." Shorty Burgess stared at his bulky, splinted arm. The hard haggard mask drew over his face again. "I just made it," he muttered. "So he brought me home. I'm obliged. Do you live here?"

"I live next door with Missus Doyle . . . and work for Pop Marcy," said Kathleen Allen briskly. "I take care of the mine books and records, and a little of everything Pop wants done."

Her eyes were blue—deep blue. Shorty Burgess stared up at them with fascination, and grinned again. "I'm your business this morning, I reckon."

"Some of it," said Kathleen Allen. "Doc Cloud will be around to see how you are. No one knows yet what happened to you last night."

"My horse went off the trail. Threw me, busted my arm, and sprained my ankle some. The norther mighty near finished me before I made it in." Shorty Burgess grinned again. "Or maybe it did get me. Maybe I died. This ain't heaven, is it?"

"Do I look like an angel?"

"You sure do."

"I see you're rapidly getting better, Shorty. But this is not heaven. I doubt if you deserve it."

That brought another hard, searching look. "Any reason for saying that, miss?"

"No," said Kathleen. "And your breakfast will be ready soon. I'll send the cook's husband to shave you. He looks like a Sonora bandit, but he used to be a barber in Chihuahua City. Then Doc Cloud will tell you when you can get up."

"He won't have much to say about it, miss. I can't stay here. I'm busted."

"Say that to Pop Marcy and he'll jump on you," warned Kathleen. "Pop says you're to be here until you're well. I'll see about your breakfast."

Shorty watched her leave the room, and then closed his eyes.

Thinking of her, Shorty wasn't sure that she'd been right about this not being heaven.

II

Two hours later, Doc Cloud loomed vastly beside the bed, dwarfing Pop Marcy at his side.

"So your horse went off the trail?" said Doc Cloud. "Which trail?"

"This side of Bottletop Pass."

Doc Cloud rubbed his chin thoughtfully. "Just ridin' through?"

"Sorta. How soon can I get up an' rustle for myself, Doc? You may as well know, I'm busted."

"Stay off that ankle for a few days."

Pop Marcy said: "You're fixed till Doc lets you up. If you want a job then, I'll see what I can rustle for you. What kind of work can you do?"

"I ain't a bad gambler. I could handle a house game one-handed. Not much else I can do right now with one arm."

"My bar don't run any steady games, son," Pop said. "Sam Clyde, over at the Thirty-Deep, has most of the play. I'll speak to Sam about you."

"I'd be obliged," said Shorty.

In five days Shorty was walking a little. The snow had melted on the south slopes, and out of the wind, the sun was warm. Pop Marcy had sent a rider up Bottle Creek, where the rocky walls hung sheerly and the snow was drifted deeply in the cañon bottom. Shorty's dead horse was drifted in down in the cañon and could not be found. Shorty had borrowed a gun from Pop Marcy.

"I don't feel dressed up without one," he had explained.

Later, Pop Marcy spoke to Doc Cloud about it. "Half the

81

loops in his gun belt was empty, Doc. He had four cartridges of one make . . . an' the rest was another make, like he loaded up in a hurry somewhere. Never said nothin' about that side wound, has he?"

"I dressed it," said Doc Cloud. "He didn't say a word. Looked me straight in the face like he was warnin' me not to ask."

Pop snorted. "He ain't foolin' no one. He was in a gunfight that took most of his cartridges. Somewheres he got him a few more, but not enough to fill his belt. Notice his eyes're mighty restless. He's watchin' for somethin'. Kathleen spoke to me about it."

"Kathleen's watchin' him mighty close," said Doc Cloud slyly. "I wonder how Nelse Halliday likes it."

"I hope," said Pop, "that Nelse loses his temper an' shows her what a skunk he really is. If she was my girl, Nelse Halliday wouldn't be callin' on her."

"But she ain't your girl," said Doc Cloud, "although she mighty near runs you. I'm wondering what this Shorty Burgess thinks about Nelse Halliday."

"You ain't the only one, Doc. I seen the way Shorty looked after Nelse hit him. I know a man when I see one. Shorty Burgess ain't the kind to forget. If I was Nelse Halliday, I wouldn't be sleepin' well now."

Doc Cloud mused: "Nelse Halliday, Kathy, and Shorty Burgess. There's a keg of powder for you."

Pop got up from the chair in Doc's office. "I'll go see Sam Clyde about a job for Burgess. I don't want Kathleen mixed up in any trouble."

Two days later, Shorty Burgess went to see Sam Clyde at the Thirty-Deep Bar.

"So you can gamble?" said Sam Clyde. "Ever been a house man?"

"Couple of times."

A big yellow diamond gleamed on Sam Clyde's right hand. His shirt was heavily striped. His heavy black mustache rolled up at the ends. "How good are you?" he asked bluntly.

"How good a man you want?"

Sam Clyde's smile was humorless. "See if you can back up your talk. Saturday nights, when things whoop up, it takes a man to sit on the lid. Buy an outfit of clothes. I'll try you out on the roulette wheel, with a helper. That's where the trouble starts oftenest. And get this. I can hire plenty of men to spin a wheel. I can get a gun-slingin' fool to throw lead into my customers. But a dead customer or a dead wheel cost me money. I need a man who can keep the wheel spinning. Pop Marcy says you're worth a try. Prove it."

Sam Clyde got a thin smile for a reply. That was all.

Lodeville knew how the stranger had staggered in out of the storm and had been knocked down by Nelse Halliday. When Shorty Burgess appeared at the roulette wheel in the rear of the Thirty-Deep Bar, men drifted closer in order to size him up.

They saw a wiry young man with a gaunt face, but he smiled easily. He ran the game in a shirt and vest, with his left arm splinted in a black silk sling. His gun was new, but his gun belt was old and scarred with use. He faced them with the impersonal manner of a veteran gambler.

Shorty knew he was on trial until the first Saturday. The five Lodeville mines paid off Saturday afternoon. Shifts closed down until Monday. Saturday came—and Shorty found that the Thirty-Deep was a crowded, roaring mecca for booted miners and cowmen. Men banked the bar and crowded the gambling tables. The roulette table had more than its share of the play.

Shorty spun the wheel, raked in the bets, and paid off with swift dexterity. And when trouble came, there was, as he had expected, no warning. A drunken miner slammed a big fist on the table.

"I played the red, damn you! Pay off! What kinda game you runnin'?"

"Place your bets," said Shorty evenly. His eyes flicked to Ben Greer, the swart, stocky, unsmiling man who was helping him.

Greer lifted a shoulder in a negative shrug.

"Hear me? You gonna pay off or not?"

The big miner leaned across the table, red with anger. His calloused hand moved back to a sheath knife on his hip.

Tense quiet dropped over the table. All eyes went to Shorty.

Sam Clyde, standing nearby, looked hastily for the two armed bouncers. They were not in sight. Sam Clyde reached to his hip pocket for the short length of lead pipe he carried on Saturdays. But Shorty was speaking calmly across the wheel.

"You had your money on the black, mister."

"You're a liar! It was red!"

Shorty's grin was cold. "You're mistaken, mister. When you play at my table, you take my say-so." Still grinning, Shorty looked at the crowd. "That goes for you all. If you play here, you take my word. Pick up your money if it don't suit you. An' I'll pull a gun on the next man who calls me a liar. This game is straight. Place your bet, mister, or get back so someone else can play. Watch the ball, gents. Here she goes. . . ."

The wheel spun. Men who had money down watched the flying ivory ball automatically—and the drunken miner glowered, muttered under his breath as he shouldered away from the table.

Sam Clyde took a breath of relief. Later he spoke to Shorty. "Good work, Burgess. You might've had trouble if you hadn't handled that drunk slick and smooth. You bluffed him without pullin' a gun."

Then Sam Clyde got a steady stare that made him blink. "Mister," said Shorty, "I don't bluff. If you want a bluffer at your wheel, go out an' hire one. While I'm runnin' the game, I'll back up what I say."

"Suit yourself," Sam Clyde yielded with a shrug. "But the first man you shoot, unless it's self-defense on your part, finishes you here in Lodeville. We've got a deputy sheriff who's hell on law an' order. You know where the back door is. The livery stable ain't far off. It's your risk."

"I kinda gathered that." Shorty nodded.

The story spread. Next day—Sunday—Kathleen spoke to Shorty about it.

"You're getting a reputation in Lodeville, Shorty. Are you really as dangerous as they say?"

They were walking together toward the mines. Shorty's sheepskin coat was belted over his stiff-splinted arm. He chuckled. "Do I look dangerous, miss?"

"You don't," said Kathleen, smiling. "But I'm just wondering."

"I wouldn't worry about it, miss."

Kathleen was silent for some moments. She looked troubled. "You never say anything about Nelse Halliday, Shorty."

"I ain't forgot him."

"It was an accident."

"I've met his kind before," Shorty said slowly. "There's only one thing they understand. I aim to teach it to the gent when I get around to it."

"You . . . you'll kill him, won't you, Shorty?"

"Maybe," said Shorty, "he'll kill me."

"I thought so," said Kathleen.

She stopped. They faced one another, and Kathleen's face was white. "You can't do it, Shorty. Nelse told me he was drinking that night. He didn't know your arm was hurt. Please forget what happened."

85

Shorty stared for a long moment. His voice was curiously flat and dead when he spoke.

"I've heard Halliday's handy with a gun. He's shot two men. They tell me he doesn't stand back when he feels like trouble. Owning the Blackbird an' Oriole Mines like he does, an' that big OTZ Ranch over in the valley, he's sure he amounts to a heap, even if he did get it from his uncle. He didn't ask you to speak to me, did he?"

"Of course not, Shorty."

"That's good enough, I reckon. I'll keep him safe for you, miss."

Kathleen bit her lip, started to say something, and then kept silent. This new Shorty was hard to talk to. An icy guard had closed about him.

Pop Marcy's curiosity continued. Pop spoke about it to Doc Cloud across a table in the Gunsight Bar.

"I've been watchin' Shorty over at the Thirty-Deep, Doc. He keeps watchin' the front door. An' it ain't Nelse Halliday he's lookin' for. I've seen him do it when Nelse was standing right there at the Thirty-Deep."

Doc Cloud expertly poured whiskey into his glass until the liquid stood a hair higher than the rim.

"Halliday ain't sure what Burgess is gonna do," said Doc Cloud. "It's gettin' under Nelse's hide."

Pop grunted. "It'll give Nelse somethin' to think about besides tryin' to buy my Gunsight Mine. I don't have to tell you how he keeps after me about it."

Doc Cloud contemplated his whiskey. "Burgess has bought a horse, saddle, saddlebags, a couple of blankets, another six-gun, an' a rifle. His outfit is cached at the livery stable . . . where a man could pick it up quick, if he wanted, on his way out of town."

"You're worse'n an' old woman at findin' out things."

Doc Cloud was unabashed. "Burgess is ready to leave. I'm bettin' he'll kill Halliday on his way out. He hasn't seein' much more of Kathleen, has he?"

"No," said Pop. "That's funny, too. They was gettin' right thick, it seemed to me."

"How's the Gunsight Mine, Pop? You been looking worried."

"It's bad, Doc. I've given orders for the men not to talk . . . but they will. The vein faulted out on us ten days ago. It'd been runnin' slimmer for a couple of months, you know."

Doc Cloud nodded.

"We lost it complete," said Pop heavily. "The bottom's outta the bucket. Nothin's comin' in. I'm borrowin' against the ranch. If we don't find that vein quick, I'm busted clean."

Doc Cloud considered. "So Nelse still wants to buy?"

"Made me another offer yesterday. Told me he knew the values had petered out."

"Funny that he still wants to buy the mine."

"The vein is around there somewhere. He must be willin' to gamble on findin' it. And so am I, Doc. But I ain't got much to gamble on. When I'm cleaned, I'll have to sell."

"Halliday's price'll be mighty slim then," guessed Doc Cloud. He poured another drink and shook his head. "Halliday isn't going to stop until he winds up owning Lodeville . . . and God help us then."

III

Five nights later Nelse Halliday came to the roulette table. His face was flushed. He had, Shorty guessed, been drinking.

Halliday's manner was ugly as he shaped a stack of gold pieces with long, nervous fingers. Men saw him and moved to the table to watch. The smoke haze over the wheel was suddenly charged with expectancy. The stacks of silver dollars, the gold pieces, the bills, and the little spinning ball were not the gamble. Trouble was in the air.

The wheel had no winning numbers for Halliday tonight. His gold pieces and chips ran out. He scrawled a check and bought more. But when he threw down the first two $50 chips, he reached out abruptly and drew them back.

"I want another man at the wheel," he stated loudly.

Men back of Halliday began to crowd away. Ben Greer looked unhappy. You couldn't handle Halliday like one of the miners on Halliday's payroll.

"Get your bets down, men . . . ," said Shorty.

Halliday pitched a gold piece across the wheel. "Here's twenty dollars to get out where I can't see you. I think you're crooked."

Shorty let the gold piece bounce to the floor. Halliday's gun arm was rigid as he stood, glaring. "Crooked . . . you sabe?" Halliday gritted. "An' I think you're a liar, too."

Shorty stared at him silently.

A sneer spread on Halliday's face. "I heard you were going to pull a gun on the first man who called you a liar."

"You're drunk," said Shorty bleakly. "But if you weren't drunk, I still wouldn't call you. I don't want any trouble with you, mister. And you can take it any way you like. Are you satisfied?"

Halliday's eyes narrowed, but he smiled with satisfaction. "I figured it was time somebody showed you up. If you ain't out of town by morning, I'll run you down the street. Drinks are on me, men!"

Ben Greer's face was a study as the crowd surged toward the bar. He spoke from the side of his mouth, not looking at Shorty. "What'n hell's wrong?"

"Nothin'," said Shorty. "Take the game. I've quit."

"Hell's fire . . . you're lettin' him run you outta town?"

"It figures up to that, I guess. So long, Ben. And good luck."

Shorty Burgess went outside. Down the street, the lights of the Gunsight Bar seemed to beam forth a welcome. . . .

Pop Marcy spoke scornfully across the Gunsight bar. "So you're lettin' Nelse Halliday run you off? I had you figured different. Your thanks for takin' you in ain't called for. I'd have done the same to a crippled dog." Pop searched Shorty's expressionless face. "Maybe," said Pop hopefully, "you're aimin' to get that arm well an' come back an' tackle Nelse."

"I won't be back this way," said Shorty.

"Nope, I reckon not. If you was man enough to tackle Nelse, you'd have done it tonight."

Pop reached angrily to set out the bar bottle. The news had spread faster than Shorty had been able to collect his pay and get over to the Gunsight.

A man at the bar sneered: "You better get goin', Burgess. Halliday told over in the Thirty-Deep that you're due for a surprise. Maybe he's comin' after you tonight. Better get your sights on the back door."

Shorty filled his glass in silence. His hand was unsteady. He was lifting the glass just when the front door opened.

A man stepped in, and two others followed at his heels. Shorty threw his usual quick look at them.

Pop Marcy and every man at the bar froze in surprise.

Shorty leaped away from the bar, dropping the whiskey glass. His gun flashed out. His crashing shot dropped the first man inside the door. The stranger's gun drove a bullet into the wall as he doubled up and fell. He'd been drawing before Shorty moved—and had been outshot.

Men were diving to safety. Pop Marcy leaned against the back edge of the bar with his eyes bulging.

Shorty Burgess was backing calmly toward the door at the rear of the bar. His splinted arm was still in the black silk sling.

A faint smile was on his face. And the big new Colt he had bought with his first pay blasted at the two bearded strangers.

Pop Marcy ducked as a wild bullet from the front smashed the bar bottle into a geyser of flying glass and whiskey.

The first man was still down, shooting from the floor. His two companions had dodged to each side of the door—and now all three were emptying their guns.

Shorty's gun *clicked* empty. He kicked open the door behind him and vanished.

Someone yelled: "Stop him! He holed that fellow without any cause!"

Pop Marcy came up with a sawed-off shotgun to challenge anyone who followed. But the two strangers still on their feet were reloading hurriedly and making no move to go after their man.

"What the hell's the idea?" yelled Pop.

"We're deputies with a warrant for that man. He's Clee Anderson, wanted for a killing. It'll take a posse now."

"It'll take more'n a posse if the three of you couldn't do it in here," retorted Pop sarcastically.

The big white snowflakes fell silently. Above the snow clouds the moon was full. Twin plumes of white vapor spurted from the nostrils of Shorty's running horse. The soft snow muted its gallop into an almost soundless throb.

Southwest, three days' ride, was the border. Shorty's splinted arm was awkward, but not painful. Gold was in the money belt next to his skin. The fresh snow would quickly cover his tracks.

Shorty grinned to himself as he turned west off the valley road. He had come south out of Lodeville, angling west toward the lower valley. If the posse missed his turn off, he'd have no more trouble. If they stuck to his tracks, there'd be another gunfight. And a one-armed man with a rifle in open country was not much good. This had been due to happen. He'd been a fool, he reckoned, to wait around Lodeville, and because he knew why he had waited, Shorty swore at himself.

Midnight was not far off. The new snow was inches deep. Ahead, the foothills still rolled down toward the lower valley. Trees were thinning out. Low junipers loomed, dark and symmetrical, under the fretwork of snow. Then the horse stopped abruptly. A wire fence barred the way.

Shorty dismounted, pulled enough staples to let the wires drop, led the horse across, and hammered back the staples with his wire cutters. You didn't leave a man's fence down if there was time to fix it.

A mile farther on, the ground fell away into a brush-rimmed draw, and a horse nickered close by as Shorty rode down the slope. Shorty reined sharply and drew his gun.

The other horse nickered again. A moment later it nosed cautiously through the falling snow, and Shorty grinned with relief. He lifted the reins and, peering hard, rode toward it as it turned away. The stirrups of an empty saddle flopped out as the horse retreated in a limping run.

Shorty caught it after a short dash. He whistled soundlessly as he pulled it up by a rein.

Snow whitened the saddle. The reins had been knotted over the saddle horn. A rifle was in the saddle boot. Shorty leaned over, and found a deep ugly furrow in the horse's flank. A bullet had done that.

The horse stood listlessly. Over to the right a small cabin loomed darkly through the drifting snow, and other horses nickered beyond it.

Behind the cabin, Shorty found three more horses in a small pole corral. The cabin was dark. Snow had drifted against the door. This meant trouble to any man's eyes.

Shorty dismounted. His horse, standing with front legs

braced, was eyeing a spot some yards to the left. There Shorty found a snow-covered man. The man was sprawled on his face, holster empty. The gun was probably somewhere close by, under the snow. The rifle in the saddle boot told its story.

This man had been shot out of the saddle without warning. The horse, burned by a bullet, had run to safety, and wandered back.

Shorty turned the body over. One eye was frozen shut; the other was wide and staring. A match limned an angular stubble-covered face that Shorty had seen before. He thought back. This man had come to Pop Marcy's house with a message. He was a ranch hand from Pop Marcy's JP Ranch. Shorty swore. This must be Pop Marcy's ranch.

IV

Shorty rolled a cigarette with one hand. The snow drifted down on the dead man's stiff face while Shorty smoked.

This was not Seguro Creek, where Pop Marcy's foreman and men could be found. This was a line cabin on the edge of Pop Marcy's ranch. The drifting snow was as white as Pop Marcy's hair, as white as Pop Marcy's heart. And a dead line rider meant trouble for an old man who had trouble enough now—if talk in Lodeville of the Gunsight Mine could be believed. Pop was back in Lodeville and a posse was scouring the country between. It would be a fool thing to try to turn back.

Shorty dragged the body into the cabin, away from prowling coyotes. He took the reins of the dead man's horse and led it as he rode west, across the wide sweep of Pop Marcy's range.

Two hours before dawn the snow stopped. As the first pale light tinted the lowering clouds, Shorty skirted a pasture fence to a wire gate. Beyond the gate a little-used road led northwest, where Seguro Creek and the ranch house must be.

He was on that winding road as the gray light brightened.

The snow was smooth ahead; far back toward Lodeville his tracks would be covered. The limping horse followed with drooping head. Shorty was half asleep, off guard as he rode around the base of a low hill.

"Pull up, feller! Don't move!"

The speaker was hidden by the brush up the slope. Shorty stopped—and three men broke out of the brush, rifles cocked. Shorty had seen two of them in town.

The first man called: "So you headed this way? Where'd you get that hoss?"

"Found him at one of the line cabins," said Shorty briefly. "There's a dead man at the cabin. I'm headin' to Marcy's ranch house to leave word."

The first man was tall and lanky; at his heels was a stocky, wide-faced man, and the two of them were trailed by a smaller man, about Shorty's size, who called: "That's Sam's black horse! Sam must be dead!"

The wide-faced man glowered as he stopped beside the road. "It ain't hard to tell who killed Sam."

The lanky man moved his rifle. "Keep them hands up! We'll take you back to Lodeville, Anderson!"

"Someone," said Shorty, "must've been out from Lodeville. I don't reckon it'd help to tell you three you're makin' one hell of a mistake."

The lanky man grinned sourly. "It won't," he said. "Let's go back to the house first, boys. Maybe some of the posse'll be back by then. Get a rope around this *hombre*'s neck, Tex, just in case he feels frisky."

They came to Seguro Creek with the rope looped around Shorty's neck and a man flanking him on each side. Gray smoke plumes rose above the Seguro Creek ranch buildings. Two windmills, corrals, and outbuildings were on the wide grassy flat beside the cold current of Seguro Creek.

Pop Marcy stepped out of the ranch house as they rode up. Consternation was on Pop's face.

"What'n hell have you men gone an' done?" Pop called. "I sent you to that line cabin . . . not to look for Shorty Burgess!"

Lannigan's reply rasped on the still morning air: "We caught him with Sam's hoss. He kilt Sam last night."

Pop spat in the trampled snow. His white eyebrows drew in a scowl. "If Burgess kilt Sam, I'll bet he had a reason. Git that rope off his neck. Come inside, Burgess, before some of that damn' posse drifts back an' sees you. Lannigan, put them hosses away. Tell the boys to forget anyone rode in here this morning."

But as they walked into the house, Shorty saw that Pop looked haggard and old. In the steaming ranch kitchen, Pop ordered an old Chinaman to start bacon, eggs, and flapjacks, and poured hot coffee.

"Set . . . an' talk," ordered Pop curtly.

Between gulps of the steaming coffee, Shorty told of his find at the line cabin. Pop stirred sugar into his coffee and stared over the cup.

"An' you headed over here to get word to me? Son, you make me feel ashamed. I ain't askin' why you throwed a gun on them jaspers in Lodeville. I've lived long enough to know a man has a reason when he cuts loose like you did last night. I tagged out with the posse to see if I could tangle your trail. They lost it . . . an' come over this way on a chance you might have headed over here to hide out." Pop drank from the cup, put it down, and sighed. "We met one of my men headin' into Lodeville. He told me we've been rustled so clean here on the ranch that the spring tally won't be worth botherin' about. Perry Jack, over at the north line camp, is missin'. I sent the boys out to see about Sam. I been runnin' the ranch short-handed lately to save money. It's busted me, I guess. I lose the mine, the Gunsight Bar, an' the ranch here as soon as the word gets out. I been borrowin' too heavy against the ranch." Pop swore softly as he lifted the cup again. "On top of that, it had to snow," he growled.

"You couldn't track a railroad engine off the place after this snow," Shorty agreed.

Pop rolled a smoke. "Son, how long had Sam been dead?"

"Hard to tell. Maybe a day or two. Maybe more. The ground was clean under him."

Pop muttered: "Cattle started then an' hazed along smart might be two jumps from the border by now. If they get acrost the valley into the breaks, an army couldn't find 'em in time to stop 'em."

Pop looked at the smoke-blackened tree trunks that held up the ceiling. He spoke absently. "I helped a Mexican put them *vigas* up there. This room was the first house. My wife was livin' in a tent back where the bunkhouse is. Some of her was built into this room. She meant a heap to me. We both worked hard to build something. She'd hate to see it go to the bank now . . . which means young Nelse Halliday. Everything we had we worked hard for. It was part of us. We built somethin'. Young Halliday don't know what that means. Everything's been handed to him on a gold platter. Son, someday you'll know the difference."

The Chinaman put down a platter of eggs and bacon. Shorty pushed the food aside. "Where are those rannihans I shot it out with?"

"With the posse, son. Two of them. The other's dead. The warrant they're carryin' says you murdered a deputy sheriff. They claim your name is Clee Anderson."

"Yeah. Burgess was my mother's name. It's good enough. They were tailing me close when I doubled back an' headed over the mountain to Lodeville. I figured sooner or later they'd look Lodeville over. I shouldn't've stayed. Six of them caught up with me over near the head of the Black River. I stood 'em

95

off until my guns were about empty, an' got away after dark. I bought some cartridges an' a fresh horse at a ranch. Spent all my money there. An' I wasn't a mile away from the ranch, up at the edge of the timber, when I saw 'em ridin' in after me. I had an idea then they'd be followin' me until hell froze over. The curly wolf I killed was one of the bunch. He drew on me when he thought I wasn't looking."

"Only three of them showed up at Lodeville, son, an' you fixed one."

"There's three more around somewhere," said Shorty without hesitation. "That bunch always hangs together. That's why I headed for the border last night. One man ain't enough to stand off a bunch of cow-thievin' killers that are on his tracks until they get him. The odds are too much to buck."

"Cow thieves?"

Shorty stared across the table. "The Blake bunch are bad *hombres*. I guess they were deputized to follow me just to get 'em outta that country. I've been wonderin' myself ever since you said your beef was gone."

"Show me a wolf track, son, an' I'll look for a kill."

Shorty nodded, and muttered: "These tracks are mixed up. I've been waitin' in Lodeville for them to show up. When they walked into the Gunsight, they came with their guns ready. They knew I was in there. They were heeled to gun me on sight. But if they'd just ridden into Lodeville, how'd they know I was there? How'd they know I was in the Gunsight right then? None of them ever knew I might call myself Burgess."

"That's somethin' to think about, son."

"Nelse Halliday spread the word I was due for a surprise last night. He seemed to know something . . . like he might've known that bunch was around." Shorty rolled another cigarette and leaned back in his chair, staring at Pop. "Nelse Halliday has been wantin' to buy your mine. Halliday owns most of the bank where you been borrowin' against your ranch. If your beef was to vanish, the bank'd get your ranch . . . an' Halliday'd get your mine."

"Son, do you think Halliday knows where my beef went?"

"If I knew why Halliday wanted your pinched-out mine so bad, I'd have a better idea," said Shorty. "Your cattle ain't been gone too long. If some of the Blake bunch made a quick roundup an' started a drive for the border, those three wouldn't have been in Lodeville last night. They'd have gone to the border with the beef, an' come back later. But if the rest of their bunch is around these parts, they must've been busy last night . . . or they'd have been in Lodeville helpin' look for me. If the posse doesn't find me, an' Orey Blake an' the skunk with him rides back to Lodeville with the posse, those two oughta be headin' out quick somewhere. If they were followed, there'd be a chance of findin' where the rest of the Blake bunch is."

The tall gaunt Lannigan entered the kitchen. "What are we gonna do about Sam?" he wanted to know.

"Sam's dead an' froze," replied Pop. "He'll keep for a little. Burgess is gonna sleep here today, an' head out tonight. If you see any of the posse an' let it out, you can pack your roll an' ride."

Lannigan shrugged. "That's plain enough."

"It better be," warned Pop. "Get a wagon an' a couple of the boys to carry Sam's body to Lodeville. I'll get some sleep myself, an' come on into town tonight."

Lannigan left.

Pop stood up. "I reckon you won't have any trouble gettin' away to the border tonight, son."

Shorty nodded. His voice went husky. "I'd most forgot there were old-timers like you left, mister."

"Git outside them eggs an' turn in," Pop ordered gruffly. "You got a heap of ridin' to do tonight."

V

The room where Shorty slept had one shuttered window, closed and barred on the inside. He had barely fallen asleep, it seemed, when a fist hammering on the door brought him out of the covers with his gun cocked.

Wood chunks had burned to white ash in the small corner fireplace. The late afternoon sun was lancing rays through the shutter chinks. The fist hammered again.

"Yeah?" said Shorty cautiously.

"It's Lannigan. The old man started for Lodeville an' said to get you ready to leave by dark. You got time to eat."

Shorty's horse had been fed and rested. Lannigan had him at the door in the early winter twilight when Shorty was ready to ride.

"Follow the creek road for about four miles an' you'll cut a trail headin' south," said Lannigan. "It'll put you the way you want to go."

"I'm obliged."

"Don't thank me," growled Lannigan. "I'd take you back. The old man's too damned soft-hearted. I'll tell him so in town tonight."

"Halliday'd be more your style, I reckon," said Shorty, swinging into the saddle.

"You didn't fool Halliday, from what I hear."

"That posse seems to have left word about everything." Shorty grinned. "Well, *adiós, amigo*. I'll see you in hell an' let the devil decide."

Shorty took the creek trail until he was out of sight, and then started a wide swing. The night chill came down. The moon was not yet up as his horse made heavy going across the open range. An hour brought him back to the traveled ranch road. The moon came up and he had clear going until he circled around Lodeville, and came into the small corral and shelter shed behind Pop Marcy's house.

The house windows were lighted. The horse nickered before Shorty could stop it. And the back door opened and Kathleen's voice called: "Is that you, Pop?"

"Come out here!" called Shorty in a low voice.

He knew by her sudden silence that Kathleen recognized him. She hurried out a moment later, wearing a small sheepskin coat, a riding skirt, and boots.

Against the gray-white snow sheen on the ground Kathleen looked slimmer, younger than ever. Her face was a pale oval against the white wool of the coat collar. When she spoke, something turned over in Shorty that he had hoped was gone for good.

"Shorty, what are you doing back here? They're looking for you. They'll . . . they'll hang you if they catch you."

"Is Pop Marcy in there?"

"No. I won't tell you where he is. Please leave."

"It wouldn't matter much if they caught me."

"It would to me," said Kathleen, and there was the faintest catch in her voice.

"You sound like you mean that," said Shorty.

"What makes you think I wouldn't mean it, Shorty?"

"I didn't know you had room to think much about anyone but Pop Marcy an' . . . Halliday."

Kathleen waited a moment before she spoke. "You've never forgotten that I asked you not to kill Nelse, have you?" she asked in a low voice.

Shorty did not try to hide his pent-up bitterness. "I did what you wanted, didn't I? He came lookin' for trouble . . . an' I backed down from him. He called me yellow . . . an' I let the town see I was yellow. Did you want more than that?"

"Shorty," said Kathleen, "you must believe me. I didn't want that. How could I know Nelse would do what he did? I thought you were the one who would make trouble."

"It doesn't matter now. Where's Pop Marcy?"

"He went to the mine with Pete Morrison, his foreman. And the posse's back. Shorty, is something wrong? Why did you come back here?"

"Because I'm a fool, I reckon. Halliday'd tell you so."

"Nelse was here about half an hour ago," said Kathleen. "One of his miners came for him. Something seemed to be wrong at the mine. He left hurriedly."

"Funny he and Pop headed for their mines this time of night," muttered Shorty. "Night shifts aren't working now. I'll go to Pop's mine."

"No," Kathleen refused. "Someone will see you. I'll go to the mine and see who's there, and meet you beyond it and tell you. Don't try to stop me."

"I'll look for you at the mine," Shorty yielded.

The shaft-head lights of the Gunsight Mine were bright points against the rising mountains beyond. To the right, not far away, lights glinted at Halliday's Oriole Mine. Beyond the Oriole, a shoulder of the mountain hid the lights of Halliday's other mine, the Blackbird.

Shorty waited in the night. He could see three horses tied near Pop Marcy's hoist house. He heard the faint *clang* of a shovel in the boiler-room. Then Kathleen's slender figure walked out on the snow and looked around. Shorty whistled softly, rode toward her.

Kathleen came to meet him. She said hurriedly: "Pop's underground with Morrison. He left this note with the hoist man, to send to me later. Shorty, I'm worried."

Shorty dismounted. "What's in it?"

"It says . . . 'I'm taking Morrison into Halliday's Oriole Mine on the old fourth level. We're heading for the sixth and seventh levels in the Oriole. If we ain't back up by midnight, better send the deputy in after us. Don't do anything until midnight."

"Gone into Halliday's Oriole Mine," Shorty muttered. "Now what's he got on his mind?"

Kathleen's small hand went to Shorty's arm. "I'm afraid, Shorty. There's trouble. Pop doesn't like Nelse. He thinks Nelse is trying to cheat him about the Gunsight Mine. And . . . and I don't know about Nelse any more. But Pop wouldn't go into the Oriole Mine this way unless something was wrong."

"Looks that way, doesn't it?" Shorty agreed, frowning.

"Pop," said Kathleen, "has been like a father to me. He's old and so alone. I can't wait until midnight. Anything might happen to him down there. Have you ever been underground, Shorty?"

"Never have," admitted Shorty.

"You don't know how it is then. You're cut off from the world. It . . . it frightens me to be under there very long."

"Does the hoist man know how to find 'em?"

"I don't think so. But Pete Morrison's brother, Tom, does. He worked in the Oriole Mine before Nelse's uncle died. He's been working in the Gunsight since then."

"Get him then," said Shorty. "I'll wait in the hoist house."

Steam was hissing softly at the hoist engine when Shorty walked into the cavernous hoist house. The engineer, wearing overalls and a grease-smudged bandanna around his neck, called a greeting—then stared when he saw who it was.

Shorty grinned thinly. "Just take it easy. Had a signal from Pop Marcy yet?"

The gray-headed hoist engineer moistened his lips, shook his head. He looked uneasily at the gun on Shorty's hip, and spoke uncertainly. "Sit down. I'm waiting for them to signal any minute."

"I'll keep standing," said Shorty. "If anyone comes, I'll get back outta sight. Got any idea why they're down in the mine?"

"They didn't say." The engineer moistened his lips again. "Folks around here figure you left these parts an' kept going."

"Which shows," said Shorty, "you can't always believe folks. Build yourself a smoke an' be easy. You got nothin' but an engine to worry about."

Shorty moved restlessly about the hoist house. Hoisting cables stretched tautly up to the crown blocks from the great cable drums and down into the mine. What a slender contact they made with the outer world.

Shorty looked over his shoulder quickly as someone rode up outside and dismounted. He was back in the shadows behind the cable drums, gun out, when a man entered.

It was the small man who had helped take him to Pop Marcy's ranch house. He came in now, and called to the engineer.

"Somebody said Marcy came here to the mine."

Shorty came out from the shadows. "Anything on your mind?"

"Hell's fire! Where'd you come from?"

"I drifted in. Why're you lookin' for Pop this time of night?"

"None of your business. But the boys are wonderin' if he's got anything else on his mind tonight before they turn in."

"You brought that body in?"

"Uhn-huh. The three of us did."

"Then round up the others," said Shorty. "Bring 'em here, with their guns. A couple of you ease over an' keep an eye on the Oriole shaft house."

"How come you're around here givin' orders?"

"I'm tellin' you what to do, in case Pop Marcy runs into trouble. It looks like he might. You ain't dodgin' trouble if he needs you?"

"Hell, no. What's wrong?"

"He'll tell you when he comes up outta the mine. Get your men here an' tell 'em to keep quiet about it."

Pop Marcy's man appealed to the hoist engineer. "What about it?"

"I reckon he knows what he's doing. The old man's down the hole."

"He better know what he's doing," was the muttered reply as Pop's man walked out.

VI

Kathleen Allen returned with a thick-chested, broad-shouldered man who needed a shave. His nod was curt. Kathleen had evidently told him what to expect. He wore a gun belt.

"This," said Kathleen, "is Tom Morrison. He knows both mines well."

"Let's get down," said Shorty.

Morrison opened a chest against the wall and began to fill his pockets with thick miner's candles. He held out a handful.

"No lights where we're going. You'll need these."

"Give me some," said Kathleen.

"Let's get started down there," said Morrison gruffly.

Kathleen walked closely beside Shorty. When he held the candle up and looked at her, she smiled uncertainly. "Like it?" she asked under her breath.

"I'd like some sky better," replied Shorty. "An' I wish you hadn't come down here."

"I couldn't wait up there in the hoist house, wondering what was happening down here."

"Kinda like Pop, don't you?"

"Don't laugh at me," said Kathleen. "I didn't come back to town while a posse was looking for me."

The tunnel roof dropped lower. Old joists and bracing

timbers had cracked, sagged. They had to climb around and over rock falls. They turned into a side tunnel, smaller and lower, so that they were bending half over as they walked. Presently there was not even that much room. Finally a wall of rock and débris blocked the way. There was barely room to crawl and inch through a narrow space over the top of loose rock.

Morrison's muffled voice came back. "We're comin' into the Oriole."

Handicapped by his bad arm, Shorty barely made it. He was panting, and his candle was almost flickering out when the loose rock gave way to a higher tunnel into Halliday's mine, where Morrison was standing with his candle.

"Here we are," said Morrison, moving on ahead.

They passed the low black mouth of a side tunnel. As yet there was no warning of danger. Then Kathleen cried: "Shorty!"

There was a rush of movement. Shorty's hand was streaking to his gun when a heavy blow from behind knocked him limply against the rough, wet rock at his side. His knees sagged helplessly. Someone brushed roughly past him, rasping: "Stand still, Morrison, damn you!"

Shorty had dropped his candle. The feeble flame was guttering out as someone caught him from behind, jerked his limp arm away from the gun, and drove him to the floor. His head struck a rock—and then his hazy impressions vanished as his candle went out. . . .

The candles were burning again when Shorty opened his eyes. He knew instantly what had happened and found he was still on the tunnel floor.

Kathleen's low, clear voice was saying: "You're lying! Of course you know what happened to them!"

In the flickering candlelight the upright figures loomed grotesquely unreal. Kathleen was there, and Morrison—and two other men. They were booted, bearded miners, and Morrison seemed to know them.

"All right, Baker," Morrison growled. "If we're in the Oriole Mine, we'll get back on our side of the line. Jumping us this way wasn't called for. It'll only start trouble, if that's what you're lookin' for."

"You was lookin' for trouble when you came," growled Baker through his short heavy beard. "You got what you asked for . . . although damned if I see why you brought the girl." Baker moved his candle. "This other one's got his eyes open. Get him up, Al."

Shorty rose to his feet, stooping under the low rock roof. He was curiously calm inside. The tomb-like rock around them might have had something to do with it.

"Halliday put you two here to watch," he said. "What's the idea?"

White teeth gleamed in Baker's black beard as he grinned. "Ask Halliday when you see him. You ought've had enough of foolin' with Halliday by now. You three come on with us."

"We might as well," said Morrison glumly. "They've got the guns."

Kathleen walked by Shorty, and spoke in a low voice: "I'm afraid for Pop."

Shorty was trying to think fast. Baker was walking ahead with a candle; the man named Al was following some paces behind them with another candle, his gun ready.

The damp rock, the blackness against which the candles feebly pushed, and the silence in which sounds were hollow and unreal made their remote world strange and depressing. Here, far underground, you could think of the open range with a fierce hunger.

They entered other low tunnels, descended old rotting ladders, crept down rocky chutes that burrowed deeper and deeper into the earth. Chances of help were vanishing behind as they were swallowed by the depths of Nelse Halliday's mine.

They were in one of the rocky chutes, descending cautiously into the pit of night below, when the sudden hollow crash of gunfire boomed beyond.

"What's that?" Morrison's startled voice whipped out. "Did you hear it?"

"Get down against the wall," Shorty said under his breath to Kathleen.

Shorty scooped a jagged piece of quartz from the floor and dived past Morrison, plunging into range of the first candle as a shout from the rear warned of his move.

Baker swung to meet him. Shorty dodged against the rough side of the chute, slamming the quartz rock as he did so. And then Baker dropped, with a crushed and mangled ear. His candle went out as the shot behind them drowned all other sounds. Shorty dived low and sprawled over the prostrate man. It wrenched his splinted arm, and he paid no attention as he groped frantically for Baker's gun.

He found the gun beside Baker's limp hand. The man called Al shot twice more in that close space. Shorty hugged the rough rock rubble and thumbed back the gun hammer. His ears rang, the sharp powder bite tinged the damp mine smell. On down in the pitch-black depths other guns were booming hollowly. Close in front of him someone was groaning.

That would be Morrison; he was wounded, perhaps dying. The blackness had a solid, terrifying quality. You could feel millions of tons of rock pressing down.

The second miner made no sound. He was there, Shorty knew, with his gun ready. He was waiting, listening, every nerve tense for a sound that would give him a target.

A choked sob nearby tightened Shorty's throat. "Shorty . . . did he shoot you?" It was Kathleen.

Carefully Shorty put his gun down and groped for a small rock. Morrison was breathing through clenched teeth, in gasps that betrayed his pain. Kathleen gulped: "He's killed Shorty."

"Keep quiet," Morrison gritted in the blackness.

Shorty got the small rock, and threw it overhead and slightly in front of where he lay—and at the same time snatched for his gun.

The sharp *click* of the rock was plain. Behind Morrison and Kathleen a red tongue of flame silhouetted a vague figure. Shorty doubled the shot blast with his own shot. He fired at the gun flame, and the man behind fell, choking. "You got me. Don't shoot. I tell you, you've got me."

Bent-legged, Shorty crept forward. Ahead of him Morrison said: "Gimme that gun, damn you, before he kills you!" A moment later Morrison added: "I got his gun! It's all right."

"I was an idiot to call to you, Shorty," said Kathleen unsteadily.

She was an arm's length away in the blackness. Shorty holstered the gun and reached for her.

"I saved Nelse Halliday for you," he said huskily. "But it's a long way up to open air. Maybe I won't see it again. I love you, Kathleen, an' I can't help it. I've wanted to tell you ever since I first met you."

Morrison's agonized protest broke in. "For God's sake, are you makin' love down in this hell hole at a time like this? I've got his gun. My shoulder's all tore up, but I'm some good yet. Let's get outta here while we got the chance. In a little while it may be too late."

Giddy from the perfume of her soft hair and the yielding of her slender body, Shorty answered. "Pop Marcy's down there, cornered. We came down to find him an' help him if he needed it. They wouldn't be fightin' if there was any idea of lettin' Pop get outta here. Kathleen, take a candle an' go back, if you can."

Morrison lighted a candle as Shorty shoved another candle and matches in Kathleen's hand. Then he turned down the chute.

VII

The booming shots down lower in the mine were intermittent now. Guns seemed to be lashing out at sudden sounds, and other guns spat quick answer.

"They're on the sixth level," husked Morrison as he followed Shorty. "Damn these echoes. You can't tell how many are down there."

They came out of the rocky chute over a rough ladder into a cross drift, and, when they emerged from the drift into a larger tunnel, the gunfire was suddenly louder. Morrison blew out his candle.

"This is the main tunnel on the sixth level."

Morrison was again leading. He knew these mines like the recesses of his mind. Shorty followed him, stumbling often, uncertain, hesitant.

The gunfire was very close now, and, as they moved closer, the firing stopped. A muffled, unnatural voice echoed along the tunnel to them.

"Dixon . . . take a man into that second drift and see if they're trying to come that way." It sounded vaguely like Halliday's voice.

Shorty bumped into Morrison, who had stopped. Crunching steps hurried toward them. Morrison's gun shattered the brief lull, and his yell rang through the tunnel. "Go after 'em, boys! Don't let 'em get away!" Morrison fired again. Shorty joined him, shouting and yelling—until the damp tunnel rang and echoed with sounds that a dozen men might have made.

Morrison was standing still. Shorty groped past him. "Come

on," he urged. "If they're waitin' for us, we might as well find it out."

The tunnel curved, and, as they followed the curving wall around, the red flame of a gunshot licked out ahead. Shorty threw a shot back at the flash. His ringing ears caught the warning shout ahead. "Here they come!"

That was all. There were no more shots. Magically the tunnel ahead was free from sound as they moved forward through a stench of powder smoke.

Morrison spoke cautiously. "Here's where they went, I think. In this drift an' up a chute . . . or around back in the tunnel, so they won't be trapped."

Close ahead, Pop Marcy's voice hailed them. Morrison answered. Pop and his mine boss joined them—and Pop Marcy swore when he discovered who was there.

"Only two of you? Burgess, you damn' fool, you shouldn't have come back here! Let's get out while we got a chance. Don't strike a light. Maybe they're waitin' for us. I know Nelse Halliday's mine as well as I do my own."

Shorty would have wandered endlessly in that maze of tunnels and drifts, but these mining men were at home in the blackness. They returned the way they had come, climbing up the chutes, the ladders, ducking under the low roofs, going unerringly from the sixth level to the fourth level—without meeting the two miners who had caught Shorty and Morrison.

A candle flame appeared ahead. It was Kathleen, waiting at the heaped rock barring the way back into the Gunsight Mine.

Pop wasted no words. "Get ahead of us, Kathleen. We're in a hurry."

They reached their own mine cage and crowded in. Pop pulled the signal rope. The cage rushed up with them. And only then did Pop admit that he was wounded.

"Got a hole through my leg . . . damn that young pup, Halliday. Old Nelse'd turn over in his grave if he knowed what was happening."

"You shouldn't have gone into his mine, Pop," said Kathleen. "Didn't you know it was dangerous?"

"I ain't afraid of Halliday," snapped Pop. "I had a hunch this afternoon why he was so set on buyin' the Gunsight. An' I was right. He cut the big vein we lost. He's been followin' it over into our rock . . . thievin' our ore! He knowed he had a sure fortune if he could buy the Gunsight. An' he'd have a heap of trouble if it got out he was tunnelin' in Gunsight rock. That's why he's been breakin' his neck with every dirty trick to buy me out." Pop swore angrily. "Old Nelse was ornery . . . but we had a heap of fun goin' after each other. It was me Old Nelse sent for when the timber caught his chest down in the Blackbird Mine an' Doc Cloud told him he had a couple of hours to live. Old Nelse give me one last cussin' out for old times' sake, an' then grabbed my hand an' told me it had been a heap of fun. He never figured this nephew they was smart enough to name after him would turn out to be so stinkin'. I didn't figure it myself, at first. But now I'll take his skin and hang it on the crown block over his shaft."

The cage stopped with a jerk and the shaft house was there before them, with the crisp night air in their faces, and the bright moon making the night silver as Lannigan and another man from Pop's ranch met them.

Lannigan was excited. "Any trouble below? Four men run this way from Halliday's mine like they meant trouble. They went back when they seen us waitin' for 'em. They just rode off a few minutes ago!"

The Morrison brother who had been with Shorty sat heavily on a box by one of the derrick timbers.

"I got to have Doc Cloud," he groaned. "I'm beat out . . . can't do no more."

"Where'd those four ride to?" Shorty asked, turning to Lannigan. "Into town?"

Lannigan shook his head, waved toward the west. "I watched 'em cut off the road just before town. One looked like Nelse Halliday but I don't know the others, nor where they went."

Shorty eyed Pop Marcy. "Gimme these men an' I'll do some trackin' after your beef."

"If you got any sense," said Pop bluntly, "you'll start for the border."

Shorty looked at Kathleen. She was pale, tired, and anxious. And she was more subdued than he had ever seen her.

"Ridin' to the border," said Shorty, "won't help me now. Catchin' your beef is the only thing that'll bring me any luck."

"It's the only thing that'll help me, son. That's the only chance I got to protect my notes. I know Halliday's stealin' my ore. But he can hogtie me with the law, hold me up, an' get his hands on the mine if I don't have some money to fight him for a coupla months. But, hell, it ain't your business. An' I ain't any good tonight to help you."

Shorty spoke to Lannigan: "How many men have you got here?"

"Three . . . an' me."

"You willin' to shoot it out, if you catch up with any rustlers?"

"You're talkin' like a damned fool!"

"Hit leather, then, an' come on," said Shorty.

They had no trouble picking up the hoof prints that cut off the road to the west. The moonlight was bright on the white snow. They rode, five of them, at an easy gallop, following the plain trail. The lights of Lodeville dropped back and vanished. Then the lonely foothills were closing about them.

Shorty breathed deeper of the cold clean air. Out here, under the open sky, a man could be himself. This was no rat hole far underground where you groped and stumbled blindly at every step.

Miles farther on the road swung west again toward the valley, and they came to a wire gate through which the four riders had passed.

When one of the men dismounted to open the gate, Lannigan said: "Nelse Halliday's south line fence, I think. I never rode up this way. Marcy men ain't been welcome on Halliday land since the old man died."

"We're bringin' our own welcome," said Shorty grimly as he rode through. "A rat runs to his hole when he gets worried. Halliday must be sweatin' to head home so quick."

His answer came in a shout that rolled down the slope at their left from bunching piñon pines 150 yards away.

"Outside the fence, you men! You're trespassin' on Halliday land!"

They were in the open, plain targets in the moonlight. Lannigan cursed under his breath.

"We're lookin' for Halliday!" Shorty called.

"He ain't here! You'll have to see him in Lodeville tomorrow! He don't say where he goes!"

"Reckon Halliday's up there?" suggested one of Lannigan's men.

On the right of the road, 100 yards away, were more trees. "Scatter out an' follow me," Shorty ordered. He spurred in a gallop toward the trees without waiting to see if they would follow. A glance back showed them coming, fanning out as they raced for cover. And on the slope beyond the road, the rifle cracked thinly against the night.

The vicious *zing-g-g* of the bullet passed close to Shorty. A second shot slapped him heavily on the left shoulder as he rode crouching. But he was still solidly in the saddle; it was only a hole through the shoulder muscles above the bad arm and he could still ride.

The rifle was barking shot after shot. One of the men yelled. Shorty looked and saw a man reining up hard and turning back. And a second man. A riderless horse was galloping on up the slope, and behind the horse a dark patch was sprawled on the white snow.

Shorty wrenched his horse around. The other rider threw himself from the saddle, holding the reins, and knelt by the fallen man.

The hidden gun spoke again. The standing horse reared, staggered, plunged down to its knees, and heaved up with a lurch.

Lannigan was the dismounted man. He was already clawing up behind one of his riders as Shorty reached the spot.

"Carson's done for!" Lannigan shouted. "Top of his head blowed off! Get up there in the trees!"

Low-hanging piñon branches crackled and cascaded snow as the men burst into the cover and came together near the top of the slope.

The shots had stopped. The third man had caught the riderless horse. Cursing, Lannigan swung onto it.

"That's one for Halliday!" he bit out. "We was warned off an' we didn't git! Chances are they'll be after us quick! Buck's dead! We ain't seen any rustlers! Now what the hell are we gonna do?"

The third man was the short, slightly-built Al, and he was resentful and angry. "This is what we get for hellin' off blind with this stranger!"

Shorty shoved a bandanna under his shirt and over the shoulder to soak up the blood. Some of his cold fury was in his comment. "Got you all whipped already, has it? Chances are we'd have got him if we'd rode straight at him. He was alone. But I didn't know but what all four of 'em were up there. You all came ready for trouble, didn't you? I put it to you plain before we started. Turnin' us back is what they want. If we circle out an' hit the road a couple of miles ahead, we can pick up their tracks again."

"An' then what?" Lannigan growled. "Bushwhacked again, an' some more of us knocked over?"

Shorty sneered at them. His shoulder was hurting; his cold fury was increasing.

"I got a bullet through my shoulder an' a sleeve full of blood. They'll tell you in Lodeville I'm yellow . . . but I'm ridin' on now. Go back an' tell Lodeville you run out when you heard a gun."

They followed him across the ridge and through the piñons on the opposite slope. A mile lay behind them when they galloped four abreast down to the shallow current of a small stream.

Ice crunched along the edge and their horses splashed into the cold current. Lannigan's sulky voice said: "Dog Creek . . . it runs into Brandy Creek down on our land."

Here Dog Creek made a long easy bend. On the inside of the bend, sand and rock formed a long flat bar that would be covered by boiling floodwater in the spring. There Lannigan stopped, pointing down and ahead. "Tracks," he said.

Shorty saw the hoof marks in the snow. "Fresh sign," he judged. "Two men. They turned off the road, I reckon."

Shorty rode to the lower end of the bar. The tracks entered the water and did not emerge on the other side. He galloped to the upper end of the bar. The tracks again entered the water, and once more did not come out on the other side. The men joined him.

"They've been ridin' up the current to kill their sign," decided Shorty. "They cut across the bend here to save time. Chances are they'll get outta the water pretty quick now. This is what we want."

They followed him again in spite of their doubts. Shorty himself was not too sure he wasn't being a reckless fool. He was losing blood. He couldn't ride on all night this way. They were on Halliday's land, and tonight Halliday was ready to kill. A dozen gunmen might be waiting ahead.

They could turn back for help, but for Shorty Burgess at Lodeville was only a hang noose. The border was far away now for a hard-ridden horse and a smashed shoulder. And Nelse Halliday might, with a little time, be able to match any moves Pop Marcy could make. Ahead was the only way to go.

They almost missed the spot where the two riders had jumped their horses out of the water onto a two-foot bank and ridden through a belt of snow-weighted *chamiso* bushes.

After that, the trail was plain in the moonlight, holding close to Dog Creek as it cut through the lower foothills. Not far away the white barrier of the mountains climbed to the high slopes where the summer range lay under deep snow. But the south slopes would again be bare after a few days of sunlight.

They were, Shorty saw, riding between two low shoulders of a mountain into a cañon where Dog Creek must rise.

The tracks swung back to Dog Creek and again entered the shallow water. Barb wire suddenly barred their way. Lannigan dismounted on the bank.

"A gate," he said. "Fixed here across the water. It's a hell of a place to have a gate."

Shorty was looking down at the skim ice by the bank. "Plenty of ridin' in an' out of here," he declared. "An' cattle have been hazed through here since the snow. This must be what we've been lookin' for. This ain't a place where anybody comes in winter. The wire holds everything that's put beyond it. What comes in an' goes out through the water here doesn't leave tracks. A man can come up the creek here for miles an' not leave any sign."

Lannigan said, as he closed the gate after them: "This is Halliday land. You don't think Halliday'd be crazy enough to throw rustled cattle back in here, do you?"

"He'd be smart enough," said Shorty "It's the last place anybody'd look. Pop Marcy thought of the border himself. He was sure his cows went south instead of north. If Pop was sure of it, who else'd think different? Halliday's got to get Pop's mine. Once he gets his hands on Pop's ranch, it won't matter where Pop's beef is. Dog Creek runs down into Pop's ranch. Hell, cattle could be drifted up the creekbed a bunch at a time, an' nobody'd ever know it. We wouldn't be here now if we hadn't cut off the road an' hit that trail across the creek bend."

"I'll have to see the beef," said Lannigan stubbornly.

Shorty swung around in the saddle, listening. "You're gonna see something quick," he said. "Riders are comin' behind us fast. Hear 'em? Get up the cañon!"

VIII

The snow had tricked them, for the thudding rumble of hoofs was closer than Shorty had at first thought. Too close. They were still in the open, plain in the moonlight, when a yell beyond the fence told that they had been sighted. Guns blasted out at them.

Over his shoulder Shorty saw a swirl of eight or ten riders boil to a stop on the other side of the gate.

Lannigan's accusing shout rang out: "You've drawed us into a hell of a fix now!"

And then they were racing up the slope beyond the creek, through junipers, cedars, and the first runty mountain pines. The chase was past the gate, stringing out after them. They were four, against twice their number, no better in these lonely mountain foothills than rabbits hunted by a yelping coyote pack. And after they were dead, it wouldn't matter much who was right or wrong. Nelse Halliday swung enough power, held enough cards to make that decision.

Three steers bolted out of the brush ahead, then two more. And then another bunch. Cattle tracks were everywhere. Half an eye could see that a big herd had been thrown on this side of the fence, higher up toward the mountains than cattle would winter.

The slope was rising. Scattered brush on the cañon floor was well below them. The horses, hard ridden already, could not keep this pace for long. If they did make a stand, they'd be ringed in, put afoot, shot down one by one.

The pursuit was slowly drawing up on them. Ahead somewhere were other men—at least the two men they had tracked. And probably more.

Lannigan spurred close. "You're ridin' into a trap, damn you!" he bawled angrily. "You know what you're doin'?"

Not far back, shots crashed out in scattered bursts as they were sighted briefly. Before there was a chance to answer Lannigan, Shorty saw the herd massed down beyond the creek on the cañon floor. Against the whiter snow it was a dark blanket, crowding in together, milling slowly and nervously as the gunfire broke the peace of the cold, clear night. Shorty saw riders down there, trying to hold the cattle together. A campfire was winking cheerfully near the base of the opposite slope.

Shorty yelled: "Hit 'em hard down there! This way!"

Down the slope he took the galloping horse. Over his shoulder he saw they were following him, and he drew his gun as he spurred harder.

They burst down out of the brush in a yelling avalanche that swept across the snow, ripped the dark creek water into turmoil, and bore down on the nervous cattle. Behind them guns barked and blasted as the pursuit followed.

Two riders moved out from the cattle, uncertain, apparently, as to what was happening. Shorty rode at them, his gun ready in his hand. He made out the dark beard of the lead man. He was close before the man jerked up his rifle.

At full gallop Shorty fired two shots at that clear target. The bearded man reeled in the saddle and his horse swerved down the cañon.

The rifle of the second rider slammed a hasty shot. It missed. Shorty's big-caliber bullet caught the horse. It lunged, squealed, and bolted back toward the stampeding cattle.

It was bound to happen—for Shorty had been riding to make it happen. The stampede started with a terrified surge of movement and grew into a snorting, bellowing rush down the cañon away from the shots and shouts sweeping out of the night. The compact mass fanned out. The deep rumbling drum of running hoofs beat out a sullen roar of sound. The cañon and the mountain slope beyond seemed to shake as the stampede gathered speed, and the outer fringe swirled around Shorty's galloping horse and gathered it in.

Any cowman knew the risk, knew what would happen if a horse stumbled and threw its rider under that mangling, stamping wave of hoofs. But the risk was no greater than the guns behind. Here in the midst of the stampede was cover of a sort. The Halliday men could only ride blindly and helplessly with that thundering wave of fear-crazed beef as it headed down out of the cañon into the lower range. Halliday had gathered a juggernaut that now was out of any control.

A grim smile flitted across Shorty's face as he gave his horse its head. Then stampeding madness was in the horse. It was running like a fresh animal, shoulder to shoulder with the surging backs that stretched out to right and left, and ahead and behind.

Back in the moonlight Shorty saw other riders who had been sucked into the stampede, and still others were galloping on the fringe, helpless to do anything but follow. Ahead, to the right, were three riders who had been watching the cattle, and they also had been caught by the rush and carried along.

The maddened cattle struck the fence, snapped all wires and swept on through the junipers and low piñons where the cañon fanned out. Trees and bushes caused eddying swirls in the main rush. One of the men ahead galloped out of an eddy not twenty yards away, swerving over so that he was recognizable. His yell was a thin whisper in the roar of sound but the red lash of his gun was plain as he opened fire.

Shot for shot they gunned it out across the tossing horns and backs, and it was not Shorty's horse that stumbled and went down.

For an instant the man sprawled on the back of a big steer. His hands were plainly visible as he frantically clawed for a hold. A thin scream came from him as he slipped down out of sight—and that was the only sound as the rushing hoofs passed over the spot.

Then the stampede began to scatter out through the piñons and broken ground, following the creek down into the lower country. Shorty worked his horse to the right. He caught sight of a rider near him, saw as they came closer together that it was Lannigan. He waved to Lannigan to bear on over to the right with him.

The bleeding shoulder was sapping strength fast. There were moments of dizziness when Shorty hung to the saddle horn with his good hand. Now the piñons were growing thicker, so that a man could not see far, but as they worked steadily toward the other side of the stampede, they sighted a rider who tried to bear off away from them. Shorty followed, and Lannigan kept with him.

They won free of the stampede. The man ahead galloped up a brushy draw. They followed him up the draw, over the rise, where it headed, and down the other slope, and Lannigan drew his rifle and fired as he rode.

The fourth shot brought the man out of the saddle. His horse stopped just beyond. He was floundering weakly on the ground when they rode up and dismounted.

Far off behind them the growing mutter of the stampede was dying away. Their spent horses were blowing heavily on the sudden quiet. Shorty staggered dizzily as he held his gun on the wounded man, who glared up at him.

"You got me. Go on an' shoot," he gasped.

"Time enough for that," said Shorty harshly. "How come Orey Blake is rustlin' for Halliday?"

"Ask Orey, damn you!"

"Orey's dead," said Shorty. "He went down in the stampede. He's deader'n that no-account boy of his'n I shot. How come you've been pullin' Halliday's chestnuts outta the fire?"

"Money, damn you. What else? We hit the ranch here one night, headin' into Lodeville, an' Orey got to talkin' to this man Halliday, an' took on a deal to help him. We needed the money, an' plenty of it was offered. Go on an' use that gun if you're goin' to."

"How bad is he wounded?" Shorty asked Lannigan.

"Not bad," said Lannigan a few moments later. "Got him in the side. Looks to me like it's tore up a couple of ribs an' come out the front. Nothin' at all."

Shorty stared back the way they had come. "Halliday's men have gone on with the stampede," he said. "Your sidekicks'll have a good chance to get away. Nothin' we can do now to stop 'em. Get this man's horse down there in the junipers an' tie him on. We got a good chance to get him to Lodeville dead or alive before Halliday's men can head us off."

"We oughta shoot him," grumbled Lannigan, but he went after the horse.

They rode through a quiet night with the prisoner riding between them. They crossed the trampled track of the stampede and no riders were visible. Beyond Dog Creek they were cloaked by the foothills until they came to the wire that was Halliday's line fence.

Lannigan cut the wire, and this time he left it down. They were back on the road not long after, riding their dead-beat horses at a walk, when they met the posse coming out. It was Pop Marcy's posse, sixteen strong. Pop Marcy was with the men, with his six-shooter and rifle.

"I was argued into thinkin', after Doc Cloud patched me up, that you men oughta be backed up. I rounded up some of my friends an' we cut the tracks an' come along. Who's this feller?"

"One of the Blake bunch," said Shorty. "Orey Blake is dead. I reckon his warrant is dead, too. It wasn't worth much, except for Orey Blake to carry it out. It was his no-account son who tried to cold-deck me with a six-shooter when I wasn't lookin', an' Orey Blake swore he'd get me for it. Orey Blake an' his men rustled your cattle for Halliday. You got Halliday where you want him now . . . an' here's one of the Blake men to give the lie to any alibi Halliday cooks up."

"Where's my cattle?" demanded Pop. "We'll go get 'em tonight!"

Shorty sagged in the saddle. "Your cattle have just about followed Dog Creek down to your land," he said. "They stampeded an' were hellin' for home the last we saw of them. You oughta find some of them waitin' at the fence. Doc Cloud is what we're needin', an' lots of him. I'll take my chance on Orey Blake's warrant in Lodeville now."

"I'll go back with you," Pop decided.

"You ain't needed. We can make it all right."

"I promised I'd get you back safe. Kathleen'd never forgive me if I lost you now. I'll take you in to her myself an' make sure. Any objections?"

Shorty grinned as he lifted the reins. "Yes," he said. "You're wastin' too much time. Let's get goin'. I'm in a hurry."

★ ★ ★ ★ ★

SHADOW

★ ★ ★ ★

T. T. Flynn married Mary C. DeRene at St. Francis de-Sales Church in the District of Columbia on May 10, 1923. Mary, who Flynn always called Molly, had been born in Baltimore, Maryland on February 12, 1897. Flynn went to work for the railroad, first as a brakeman, and then got a job in a roundhouse. It was at this time that he first began to write fiction. When Flynn was fired from his job in the roundhouse for writing on company time, he decided no one could write part-time. It had to be a full-time vocation, or none at all. Living in Hyattsville, Maryland with Molly, Flynn continued to work capably and quickly at stories with a variety of different settings, but predominant at this time are railroad backgrounds in much of the fiction published under his byline in *Short Stories* and *Adventure*. Molly suffered from tuberculosis and so Flynn took her to New Mexico because the climate was reputed to be good for those afflicted with lung disorders. She suffered terribly before she died in Santa Fé on August 11, 1929. The perceptive reader might deduce that Flynn had witnessed her passing since his descriptions ever after of death in his fiction could only have been written by a man with first-hand knowledge. There are no grimaces or grins on his corpses, only the frozen vacancy, the terrible silence, the pallor as the blood vanishes from the surface of the skin. Molly Flynn's death certificate does not provide a description of her, but Walt Coburn, who had met her, did so in his short novel, "Son of the Wild Bunch," in *10 Story Western* (10/36). In this story Pat Flynn, after the death of his wife, leaves their infant son, Jimmy, with Iron Hand and his wife to raise. Jimmy asks Iron Hand's wife what his mother was like, and she tells him: "The most beautiful woman she had ever seen, with blue-black hair and dark blue eyes. Pat Flynn had called her Molly. She had been young. The squaw had picked a wild rose, just out of bud, and had held it out to the boy. 'Like that,' she told Jim." "Shadow" is one of those early railroad stories, appearing in *Adventure* (7/23/26).

His mother named him George Washington Archibald Macgilli-cuddy. When Spreckles, the D&R road foreman of engineers between Rawlings and Mountain City, took a long chance and signed him on as a fireman, he gave his name as George Macgil-licuddy. But the first time he shambled into the crew dispatcher's office, Kelly, fireman on the Hill and Plain Express, took one look at his long, gangling, incredibly thin form and dubbed him "Shadow". And Shadow Macgillicuddy he became the rest of his natural life.

Shadow was tall and lean and, when viewed from the side, he did look something like the thin edge of a shadow. His head was crowned with red hair, and great freckles splotched his face and neck and arms. His eyes, a washed-out blue, surveyed the world half timorously, half wistfully, and always cheerfully.

When the Macgillicuddys located in Rawlings, Shadow was the proud father of five bouncing, bawling, and exceedingly troublesome youngsters. Five years later, when he had gradu-ated from the extra list and was firing local freight, he was the prouder father of nine.

In those five years Shadow had become part and parcel of the D&R. He was a born railroader, and every inch of his six feet two, every pound of his 153 were attached to the road with a fierce loyalty. He knew it was the best road in the country, had the fastest locomotives, the best officials, the greatest heritage of pride, and he was almost humbly glad to be granted the favor of working on it.

Confidently he wove his future with that of the road. The years stretched away, an ever-brightening path leading to an engineer's seat in a yard engine, a freight engine, and finally a fast passenger engine, with the prestige and fat pay check that went with such glory. And at the end was the safe haven of a pension from the company and a final life of indolent ease, ending only in the grave. To Shadow's way of thinking, a man could wish for no more, and in his fifth year at his job he was well on the way to his desire.

Shadow's fifth year on the D&R was an off year and his household was not gladdened with an addition. But, early in his sixth year of service, Nature, apparently regretting her niggardliness of the year before, bestowed triplets upon the clan of Macgillicuddy.

It was an epic event. Shadow almost burst with pride when the news was brought to him by the harried midwife. After a palpitating inspection of the new arrivals and the assurance that the rest of his round dozen were being looked after by the neighbors, Shadow proceeded to get gloriously, thoroughly, and completely soused.

That yearly inebriation was a fixed habit, almost a rite. In a manner of speaking it was Shadow's way of baptizing the new arrival into the home circle. As such, it was accepted by everyone. What mattered if Shadow did stretch things a little on that occasion? The time, for instance, when he wandered down to the ready lot, commandeered a yard engine, and announced his intention of racing the Hill and Plain Express to Mountain City with it. And the year Woodrow Wilson Macgillicuddy made his advent into the world, when Shadow visited the roundhouse and, finding the turntable operator absent, tried to make a merry-go-round out of the turntable. Such things could be eyed tolerantly in view of the event and the generally excellent record

Shadow made the rest of the year.

But even as the triplets bulked over the usual yearly arrival, so did Shadow's alcoholic celebration tower over former ones. Some of it may have been due to the vile concoctions he was obliged to accept for liquor, but there was no denying his enthusiasm. At that, things would have been all right if fate had not elected to play a hand.

Daniel Weegan, austere president of the whole D&R system, was making an inspection of the entire road. Jim Ryan, the heavy-set, iron-jawed superintendent of the Mountain Division, was conducting Weegan and his party over the division. For weeks preparations had been made for the visit. The roadbed was clean and orderly, buildings were newly painted, all scrap collected, old ties burned, the yards cleaned up, and at Rawlings the roundhouse, the back shop, and their attendant buildings were gone over as with a fine-toothed comb.

Ryan and Blanton, the Rawlings master mechanic, met the inspection party when they came on the Mountain Division at Rawlings and conducted them over the Rawlings property. All went well until they entered the roundhouse. Halfway through it they stopped by the side of a great mountain freight engine and listened while Blanton pridefully told them what a fine, upstanding bunch of men were on the Rawlings payroll.

"As fine a lot of fellows as you'll find on the whole road, Mister Weegan," he said enthusiastically. "There's not a man among them who is not a sober, steady worker, who wouldn't go to the last ditch for the D and R."

Daniel Weegan stroked his beard and nodded approvingly.

Spreckles, the road foreman of engineers, who was with Ryan and Blanton, added his bit. "It's true," he said feelingly. "We have reason to be proud of every one of them."

"I like that," Weegan said heartily. "Our road is built on men, gentlemen. We can lay down the best steel, purchase the finest rolling stock, and furnish the best equipment on the market. But if we haven't the men, we won't have a road worthy of the name. Keep at it, weed out the unfit, treat the fit well, and we'll go far."

Ryan nodded. "There's none but fit on the Mountain Division," he averred. "To the last man they are a credit to the road."

Weegan nodded again, and, when Ryan saw it, he lifted the corner of his mouth at Blanton. There was little doubt that the Mountain Division was making a noble impression upon Weegan and the high officials who accompanied him.

Weegan turned to Ryan and spoke, but his words were overwhelmed as the bell of the freight hog beside them suddenly broke into wild clamor. Weegan halted his remarks and frowned.

Ryan's face grew red, and Blanton, with a muttered curse, made for the cab of the engine. Before he reached the cab steps, the whistle of the freight hog cut loose in a blast, and then the lanky form of Shadow Macgillicuddy leaned out the window. He was wildly drunk and clutched a pint bottle, half full, in his right hand. He waved the bottle at Blanton and at the group and broke into song.

Weegan looked at Ryan. Ryan purpled under the glance and said to Spreckles thickly: "That man . . . who is he?"

Spreckles shifted uncomfortably, but it was no time to be saving other men's shirts. His own was in danger, for a road foreman doesn't bulk very large in the eyes of the superintendent. "I think it's a fireman, a man named Macgillicuddy."

"Think?" asked Ryan savagely. "Are you paid to think who the men under you are?"

"Well, I know," said Spreckles.

"Ha!" snorted Ryan, and looked at Blanton.

The master mechanic had stopped beneath the cab window

and was glaring up at Shadow Macgillicuddy.

"You're fired!" he roared savagely.

Shadow leered at him. "Fired!" he whooped. "Me fired! Wh'd I care. Tr'pl'ts!" He pulled on the whistle cord again, and then waved the bottle at the party of officials. "Drink!" he urged hospitably. "Drink t' tr'pl'ts!"

Weegan, a noted dry, swelled with indignation. Ryan, seeing the careful plans of weeks being destroyed, gritted his teeth in suppressed fury.

Shadow broke into discordant song again, but before he had a chance to sing more than several bars, thunder, in the shape of Blanton, struck him. The master mechanic, driven by a fury equal to Ryan's, had scaled the cab steps, stepped behind Shadow, reached forth a long arm, plucked him bodily from the cab seat, and jerked him back into the cab.

"You're fired!" Blanton cried, shaking the lanky form of Shadow until the faded blue eyes almost popped from their sockets.

The small matter of being fired or hired was of little import to Shadow Macgillicuddy at that moment. He giggled hugely and again essayed to sing.

Blanton, seeing that drastic action was necessary, hauled him down from the cab on the side away from the party and, hustling him away from the immediate vicinity, turned him over to a couple of machinists with rapid instructions to throw him off the property and keep him off.

But the damage was done. Weegan's visit to the Mountain Division, the visit that was to have been one triumphant, smooth tour, was flatter and cooler than a cold fried egg. When the presidential party passed over into the next division, it left behind a dank chill cloud of gloom and a violent antipathy in the breasts of Spreckles, of Blanton, and of Ryan toward all who bore the name of Macgillicuddy. Which wouldn't have been so bad had there only been Shadow to consider. But there was Mrs. Macgillicuddy and twelve hungry youngsters in the offing.

By the next morning Shadow was sober, and he didn't remember that he had been fired. Blessed forgetfulness had wiped the painful scene from his mind, and, secure in the tradition of former years, he reported for work.

Shadow got clear into the crew dispatcher's office without being acquainted with the fact that he had no job. He was gay in spirit, considering the hang-over that he had awakened with that morning, and he breezed through the door of the dispatcher's office, whistling a little ditty, and nodded to the men who were standing around inside.

"Howdy, men," he said gaily. "I suppose you've all heard of me good luck."

A silence fell over the room when the men saw who it was. To a man, they knew of the happening the day before and the black trouble that had descended upon the house of Macgillicuddy. They shuffled their feet uneasily, and none had the courage to answer Shadow.

He blinked and looked at them wonderingly. "And have none of you heard I have triplets at me house?" he asked after a moment.

Not a man spoke.

Finally Henderson, the engineer who been assigned to the Hill and Plain Express after Pop Hand retired, spoke up gruffly: "Aye, Shadow," he said gruffly. "There's not many could do it. An' it had to happen to a starved-lookin' galoot like you."

Shadow chuckled and the tension was broken. "Results is what counts," he reminded them. He straightened his long lean form, thrust out his flat chest, and swaggered over to the rail before the crew dispatcher's desk. "Here I am, Joe," he said cheerfully. "Mark me up, will you? I have need for much work, what with the increase and all."

Joe, the crew dispatcher, hesitated, and then passed the buck. "I . . . I think Spreckles wants to see you," he told Shadow.

"Spreckles?" Shadow wrinkled his brow thoughtfully, looked at Joe, and then around at the boys. "Now what could Spreckles be wantin' me for?"

No one said a word.

Shadow looked at them and grinned. "Maybe he's going to praise me for the triplets bringing distinction to the Mountain Division," he suggested. "They's none o' you has come to the front with such a contribution."

He favored them with a cheerful grin, and left the room jauntily. For what could Spreckles want save to extend congratulations or impart good news?

Spreckles was in his office, his nose buried in a report, when Shadow entered. He did not see who it was until he looked up and stared fully into Shadow's grin.

Shadow spoke first. "Howdy, boss."

Spreckles's face grew red and he swelled visibly. "Well?" he asked after a moment of silence.

"Joe said you wanted to see me," Shadow explained, and he twirled his shabby work hat on the end of his finger as he spoke.

"Want to see you?" Spreckles spoke as though the suggestion were anathema. "No," he gritted, "I don't want to see you . . . ever!"

Shadow stopped the gyrations of his hat and looked at Spreckles in astonishment. He sensed that there was something decidedly wrong in Spreckles's attitude. "Well, Joe said so," he finally replied uncertainly.

"What are you doing here anyway?" asked Spreckles irritably. "What were you talking to Joe for?"

Shadow stared at him, puzzled. "I came to work. I went in Joe's office to get him to mark me up."

"Mark you up?"

Shadow nodded.

A thought came to Spreckles. "While you are here, I'll fix you up," he said.

He reached into the drawer of his desk and pulled forth a pad of slips. While Shadow waited, his hat swinging uneasily on the end of his finger, Spreckles wrote. With a final jab of his pen he finished, blotted the paper, and tore off the sheet on which he had written.

"There!" he said, tossing it across the desk. "There's the order for your time. Get it and beat it off the property quick. I don't want to see you."

Shadow gaped at him with his mouth open. His hat slid off the finger, dropped to the floor, and lay unnoticed.

"My time?" he echoed.

"Your time?" confirmed Spreckles.

"Wh-why," stammered Shadow, "what are you giving me my time for?"

"It's the custom," said Spreckles sarcastically. "When a man is fired, he gets his time."

"Fired?"

"Damn it, yes! Fired! Can't you understand plain English?"

"But," said Shadow painfully, "what are you firing me for? What have I done?"

"What have you done? *Arggggh!* What haven't you done?" Spreckles growled. "That's easier to answer."

Tiny beads of sweat came out on Shadow's forehead.

"What is it?" he begged. "Tell me."

Spreckles looked at him sharply and asked: "You don't know?"

"No."

"Not a thing?"

"Well," said Shadow painfully, "I got lit up a little yesterday.

The missus had triplets, you know, an' I sort've had to blow off a little steam. But I got time off, and I wasn't drunk on duty. I have done it every year since I have been working on the D and R and no one has said there was any harm in it."

Spreckles leaned back in his chair and looked at Shadow. "You didn't remember a thing when you sobered up?"

"No," said Shadow, "not a thing."

"Well," said Spreckles, and he shook his head feelingly, "you sure played yesterday." He lit a cigar and proceeded to acquaint Shadow with every detail of the day before. "And," he finished, "you're fired as high as the Eiffel Tower, and that's all there is to it."

Shadow took it quietly, but his faded blue eyes darkened with the dread of the days that lay ahead—jobless days, moneyless days, hungry days for him and for his family. He touched his lips with the end of his tongue, swallowed once or twice, and then spoke a trifle huskily. "An' then I'm really fired, Mister Spreckles?"

"You are," said Spreckles positively. "And be thankful that you have your life. There was near murder done yesterday. You have given the whole Mountain Division a black eye."

Shadow stooped, picked up his hat, and turned the faded brim nervously in his fingers. He started to speak, and then said nothing.

Spreckles, who was a kindly man at heart, spoke further. "You are through on the D and R, Macgillicuddy. It would be worth my job, if Ryan ever saw your name on the payroll again. You had best pack up and move somewhere else. I know it's hard, a man with a big family and all. But you put your foot in too deep this time."

Shadow swallowed and nodded. "All right," he said, and his voice came huskily, as if his throat was swelled almost shut. "All right, I'll try to make out somehow."

He clapped his old hat on his head, took the discharge slip, and made for the door, and such was the blow he had been dealt that he collided with the side of the door, unseeingly, as if he was still half drunk.

In the days that followed Shadow tried to make out somehow. He remained in Rawlings, partly because he had no money to move away, partly because it was home. In Rawlings his roots were buried deeply in the soil of familiarity. There, also, was his railroad, for the D&R was still his road. The fire of loyalty that had blazed with increasing intensity in Shadow's flattened chest still burned highly. He was divorced from the company rolls, but his spiritual contact was not broken. To him the D&R was still the finest stretch of steel in the country, and he was a part of it. He felt no animosity toward Ryan, Blanton, or Spreckles. He realized that he had acted in a manner ill befitting one who belonged on the D&R and felt the disgrace he had brought on the Mountain Division almost as fully as did those who had discharged him. Feeling as he did, he remained close by that which had cast him off, obtaining in his groping way a measure of comfort from proximity to that which might have been.

His way was hard. There were no factories in Rawlings. Nothing but the railroad and such businesses as catered to the railroad men and the farmer folk in the country roundabout. Shadow sought work futilely and with increasing despair. When it seemed as if every possibility had been exhausted, he shambled into the grocery store of Abe Gatz and was hired to deliver groceries. The salary was small, for Abe Gatz was not the man to pay much money for anything and certainly not for something that most boys could do. Still, it was work, and Shadow clutched at it with the desperation of the jobless. It was something with which to battle the specter of want that had suddenly reared up into his life.

Every morning at six Shadow reported for work. All day he

sat on Gatz's rickety wagon, clucked to the bony old horse, and carried boxes of groceries into back doors. In addition he kept the store windows clean, swept out the store, put up orders, carted freight from the station, and kept the horse and stable clean. But, although Shadow had a job, he also had fourteen mouths to feed on less than half what he had earned on the railroad. He began to wear a haggard look. After Gatz closed the store at six in the evening and Shadow was free, he often did odd jobs, such as cutting lawns, burying trash, and sawing wood against the winter months to come.

The Macgillicuddy children grew scrawny and ragged. John, the oldest, worked for Gatz every Saturday. His brother, a year younger, obtained the Rawlings agency for several magazines. Their income must still have been deficient, for one day one of the children was seen hauling wash home on the little wagon that Shadow had bought him in their more prosperous days. Game, plucky little Mrs. Macgillicuddy was much smaller than Shadow, with the burden of twelve children on her shoulders, many of them infants. Yet such was their need that she had to take in washing to keep bread in their mouths and milk in their bottles.

That washing must have been cruel for Shadow. He loved his wife with all his simple heart, and the thought of her adding washing to the rest of her cares bore down upon him heavily. His face showed it. It grew wan and pinched and deep lines became etched where once had been wrinkles of laughter. He tried desperately for other work that would pay more, but it simply was not to be had for love or money.

His plight was not unknown to Blanton and Spreckles. No man's state can long be hidden in a community the size of Rawlings. Shadow delivered groceries to Blanton's back door, and occasionally Blanton saw him and noted the ravages of circumstances on his pinched face.

One day Blanton and Spreckles were walking home together when they passed one of the Macgillicuddy children struggling with a load of wash. The little wagon was wedged in a rut, and the frail strength of the youngster was inadequate to free it.

Blanton stopped, lifted up the wagon, and set it on smooth going once more. After the youngster had thanked him gratefully and trundled off with his burden, Blanton stood in his tracks and looked after him with a frown.

"That family is having the very devil of a time to make ends meet, Spreckles," he said. "Did you notice the shoes that kid has on? I saw his father the other day, and his own feet were shod no better."

"It's hard," agreed Spreckles, and he added: "Were it up to me, I would give the man back his place. What is done, is done. He's had his lesson, and he always was a good steady worker."

"Yes," said Blanton, falling into step beside Spreckles once more. "If it was up to us, it would be all right. But it's not. Ryan sat in on this deal. If Macgillicuddy went back on the payroll and Ryan found it out, good night. You know Ryan."

Spreckles nodded. He did know Ryan. Every man on the division knew Ryan. If a man did his part beyond censure, Ryan was all right, a fair and just man in the main. But let a man once fall, succumb to carelessness, neglect, let him do something out of the line of duty, and Ryan became stern and implacable. He had no use for the man who was not a smooth, efficient cog in the scheme of things. No. As far as Ryan was concerned, the thing was over for all time, and to seek to reopen it would be an extremely foolhardy act. Blanton and Spreckles let the subject drop.

Autumn dragged to a bleak end. The green leaves of summer gave way to flaming colors and, in turn, withered and fluttered to the ground. The days became crisp and the nights cool. And with the demand for winter clothes, for coal and the increasing appetites of the growing children, the Macgillicuddys were forced to retrench further. The rent was the only place where the pruning knife could be applied. So they moved from the comfortable house they had occupied since they first came to Rawlings, moved to a veritable shack down near the roundhouse, where the rent was negligible.

The sacrifice had some compensations for Shadow. They were near the railroad. Of an evening when he had no work to do, he would sit on the front porch and listen to the activities of the shops. To his ears came the roar of the blowers, the crash of iron mauls against the side of coal tipple cars, the *rat-a-tat* of boilermakers' air chisels, the whistles and bells of arriving and departing engines, and the pop and rush of escaping steam from locomotive safety valves. It all blended into a soothing cadence that was the sweetest of music to Shadow Macgillicuddy.

If he cared to do so, and he often did, he could walk a half a block and come out beside the main line tracks. There on a bank he would sit and smoke his stubby black pipe and watch the long freights rumble past, and the passenger trains as they came out of Rawlings and picked up speed for the run to Dickson at the foot of Twenty Mile Grade. On the engines were men he knew, and often they waved at him. He waved back and watched them thunder off into the distance with a wistful look in his faded blue eyes. After such an incident Shadow would sigh heavily and sometimes dream for a few minutes and sometimes uncoil his long, lanky form and shamble home to his brood and some task that remained to be finished.

December came, and with it the first snow and cold of the winter. Shadow still delivered groceries for Abe Gatz. It was cold work. Even with the retrenchment there was little money for clothes in the Macgillicuddy exchequer, and Shadow was thinly clad against the chill blasts. But he perched on the rickety wagon bravely and continued to make his smiling rounds despite wet, half-frozen feet and chill flesh. Sometimes, although the bank alongside the railroad track was covered with snow, he found time to slip away in the early darkness and watch the trains pass for a short time.

In the middle of December the first heavy gale of winter arrived. It swept down out of the northwest, howling, shrieking, driving half snow, half sleet in cutting sheets across the landscape. Fortunately it did not arrive until late afternoon when Shadow was almost through with his deliveries. But at that he was blue with the cold when he returned to the store. He drove the horse into the barn without stopping to unload the empty delivery boxes. His teeth chattered and chills raced through his body. He could think of nothing save the warm stove in the store.

His fingers were so stiff with the cold that he could hardly unbuckle the harness straps. But finally he stripped the harness off and flung it over the harness rack. Before he went into the store, he threw fresh straw under the horse, carried water for him to drink, and filled his feed box. Not until he was sure that the dumb beast was comfortable did he leave the barn.

The red-hot stove in the store was a thing of joy. Shadow stood by it, soaking up the heat until his worn clothes smoked and became painfully hot. It seemed as if he would never get warm enough. Finally Abe Gatz spoke sharply from behind the counter.

"The floor iss very dirty, yess?"

Shadow nodded wearily and went for the broom. Gatz kept him busy until six o'clock. Shadow was almost grateful. He dreaded the thought of the walk home through the storm. But at last Gatz unwound the strings of his soiled apron from about his fat middle and emptied the contents of the cash drawer into a dirty salt sack. Another day was over and Shadow, hugging the stove until the last minute, finally found himself on his way home.

Darkness had fallen, and he stumbled and slipped in the mounting drifts. It was cold, bitterly so. He shivered and hugged his arms tightly against his thin body in a futile effort to keep out the wind and hold in some of the body heat. He passed the comfortable house that they had been forced to vacate and plunged on toward the little place where they were living. At least it would be warm. They were close to the railroad and the children had picked up much coal from along the tracks.

The houses thinned out, and presently Shadow was wading knee deep in unbroken drifts. At last he saw through the darkness the lights of his little place. Back of it, shining dimly through the darkness and the falling snow, were some of the roundhouse lights. Shadow looked at them as he plodded forward. They were symbols of a safe haven. Beneath them was steady work, good wages, a care-free life, and agreeable companions. Regret that he was barred from them, a wave of homesickness for a warm cab, the smell of coal-gas smoke, of hot oil and steam swept him.

Just before he reached the front gate, he heard above the howling wind the crashing exhaust of a great freight engine laboring along the main line. It called to him in a language that he knew and understood. He shivered in the icy blast and thought of the cab of the engine. The storm curtains were down, he knew, and the cab windows closed. It was warm and cozy inside and the fireman was sitting back at his ease, for the freight engines of the D&R had automatic stokers on them that fed coal on the fire with no effort on the part of the fireman.

Shadow stumped up his front walk to the porch and tramped the snow from his feet. In spite of the cold and the lure of the warmth on the other side of the door, he stopped for a brief instant to listen again to the measured beat of the freight train's progress. He heard this, and something else, as he stood with his senses sharpened and listening. Through the storm, over the noise of the passing train, he heard the whistle of the shops rise in a long, wailing blast.

Shadow stiffened and listened intently.

The door beside him opened and Mrs. Macgillicuddy peered out. She had heard Shadow's footsteps and wondered at his delay in entering. When she saw him standing there, peering off into the storm, she spoke sharply: "George! What's the matter with you? Come in here out of the storm!"

Shadow shook his head and motioned for her to be quiet. The next instant the whistle came again and again. Smothered by the storm, overwhelmed by the noise of the passing freight, nevertheless it came clearly to his straining ears. It was the fire signal at the shops. Fire, and a gale blowing. It could easily be a terrible thing.

Shadow turned. "Fire!" he exclaimed excitedly. "There's a fire at the roundhouse!"

Mrs. Macgillicuddy sniffed. She shared none of Shadow's love for the railroad. If anything she felt resentment against it. Much of their straitened circumstances she laid at the door of the railroad, and any reference to it was liable to provoke a hot reply. As she saw her husband standing out in the storm, felt her house getting cold from the door she held open for him, and then heard him begin to talk about the railroad, her wrath boiled over.

"What of it?" she demanded sharply. "What's the railroad to you? Come in out of the cold. The house is getting all chilled off."

Shadow stared intently in the direction of the shops and said nothing.

"George Macgillicuddy," said his wife ominously, "you come in here!"

Shadow came unwillingly and slowly, but he came. In their house there was one ruling spirit, and it was not Shadow.

Mrs. Macgillicuddy bustled back into the kitchen, voicing her opinion of a man who would stand out in the storm mooning over a company that had fired him. Shadow paid her no heed. He prowled restlessly about the living room with his coat still on. A dozen turns he made, and then, with a guilty look at the door leading back to the kitchen, he opened the front door a trifle and applied his ear to it. The freight was dwindling away in the distance, the noise of the storm arose louder, and of the fire whistle there was no sound.

Shadow closed the door and again took up his restless pacing. There was a fire at the roundhouse, he knew. It might be small. It might be large and getting larger. In any event he felt that he must go to it. Not just because it was a fire, but because it was a fire on the railroad—his railroad. In spirit he was still a part of the D&R, and, when danger or trouble threatened, he felt it his duty to answer.

Dishes rattled in the kitchen. The children's voices rose in a hum of conversation. Presently Mrs. Macgillicuddy spoke.

"Supper is ready, George. You can wash and set down."

Shadow stopped his pacing and, after a moment's hesitation, started for the kitchen door. Halfway to it he stopped and, on an impulse, went to the window, pulled the curtains aside, smeared a peephole in the frosting on the glass, and peered out into the night. What he saw made him forget the supper, forget his wife, forget his weariness, his damp feet, his recent chills that had hardly left him. Through the falling flakes of snow a red glow was rising over the shops. As he stared, it increased, and a swirl that might have been smoke and might have been snow shot up from it.

Shadow let the curtains fall back in place and stood undecided. It was a big fire. They would need every man they could get, and more. In common decency he should go. His hat lay on the chair by the front door where he had dropped it when he came in. He took a step toward it.

Mrs. Macgillicuddy called from the kitchen.

"George! Supper is on the table. The children are all seated and waiting on you. Are you ever coming?"

Shadow picked up his hat and grasped the doorknob in his hand. He took a deep breath. "Not hungry!" he called. "They's a big fire over at the shops. I'm going to run over and see if I can help any. Can't run any risks of letting it get out of control, you know. It might get over into the town."

Without waiting for her reply, he opened the door and plunged outside. Jamming his hat tightly on his head and ducking into the blast, he ran down the front walk and out the front gate. As he struggled through the drifts toward the shops, the glow grew brighter. He came to the edge of the roundhouse yards. Over the top of a line of coal cars darting flicks of flame became visible, apparently coming from the machine shop.

The line of coal cars blocked the way and Shadow was forced to climb between them or make a long detour around the end. He chose to climb. Such was his haste that he struck his knee on the coupler cut lever as he clambered through. The pain was intense, but he dropped to the ground on the other side and continued without stopping, limping as he ran. He crossed the last line of tracks, ran under the coal tipple, and burst out by the fire.

It was as he had thought. The machine shop, a great brick-walled building, holding the machine and carpenter shops, was in flames. Shadow was at the rear, behind a small building, or rather vault of brick, which had been added to the machine shop the year before to conform with new state laws relative to the storage of oils and other explosives. The walls of the building were of brick. The fire was inside. Many of the tall windows filling the brick walls were broken and vomiting smoke and bursts of sparks. The entrance was on the other side, and Shadow hastened there.

He found a motley crowd at the front of the machine shop. There were half naked boilermakers, fresh from the sweltering fire boxes of hot engines, machinists bundled in greasy clothes, engineers and firemen, some of whom had been asleep in the bunk room and had dashed out into the night half dressed at the first alarm. And there were several men, clean and well clothed against the storm, who had just reported for work.

Kent, the four to twelve foreman, was in charge. He had managed to have a hose run from a nearby fireplug and several men were directing the stream of water through one of the front windows. The one stream was of little effect against the fire. The floor of the machine shop was of wood. There were wooden racks and benches scattered all about. In one corner a two-storied tool room and office was constructed of wood. At the other end of the building was the carpenter shop. It was filled with wooden benches, piles of shavings and wood scraps, and large racks of wood. Everything was soaked with the oil and grease drippings of years.

Both ends of the building were afire. The floor of the machine shop, the wooden tool room, and the office above it were covered with licking flames. The racks of wood in the carpenter sections were blazing and the wooden roof overhead was afire. The entire inside of the huge building was a mass of smoke, sparks, and crackling flames.

Kent, seeing that one stream was having little effect on the fire, turned to the men who clustered about the entrance.

"Let's get some more hose!" he shouted. "There's some in the roundhouse. Come on!"

A dozen men followed him, and Shadow was at their head. His thin frame was once more shaking from the cold, his feet were numb, his hands so chilled that they hurt. But the fire of his loyalty to the road blazed highly within him and he felt nothing. His hand closed on the end of the reel of hose just behind Kent's. Still limping from the blow on his knee, panting heavily from his exertions, he followed Kent back to the fire with the end of the hose. Kent stopped at the plug to which the other hose was attached. On the plug was a pipe for another hose.

There was a wrench hanging from the plug by a chain. Kent seized it and hurriedly unscrewed the cap over the second pipe. It came off, and the cold water burst forth. Shadow, who knelt before it with the end of the hose, was drenched. Kent had forgotten to shut the water off while the new hose was being attached.

Shadow leaped to one side with a howl. But in spite of his quick move he was soaked.

"Damn it!" he cried, dancing around with chattering teeth. "Whyn't you watch what you are doing? Gimme that wrench!"

He seized the wrench from Kent's fingers and shut off the water.

There was no time to argue. As soon as the stream slackened, Kent jammed the end of the new hose on the pipe and screwed the coupling tightly. Still swearing through chattering teeth, Shadow reached down, gave it the last few turns with the wrench he held, and then turned on the water once more.

The limp hose stiffened and straightened like an angry snake as the water rushed through it. One man held the nozzle of the new hose, and he grasped it carelessly. When the water reached the nozzle, it flicked from the man's hands and writhed furiously over the ground, showering water on all sides. The men scattered from the cold stream.

Shadow, wet, freezing in the icy wind, saw the nozzle flick from the man's grasp and go free. He saw the men run from the flying water. At the sight his feelings boiled over.

"Damn it!" he shouted again. "Ain't anybody got any sense?"

He charged along the line of hose, butted a man out of the way, and cast himself fully upon the writhing end. He came up in a minute, gasping, spluttering, every inch of his body soaked and dripping, but with the nozzle under control. He wrestled with it in a mounting anger.

"Come here!" he bellowed at the men. "Give a hand! Are you afraid?"

Seeing the water under control, several men rushed forward and helped to hold the nozzle. Shadow led them forward until they were standing in the doorway of the burning building. The heat from the inside was uncomfortable and the swirling clouds of smoke surrounded them. The man next to Shadow shrank back and began to cough from the smoke.

"It's hot," he choked.

Shadow grinned at him. "Hot, is it?" he howled. "And so's another place. You might as well get used to it."

He deliberately took another step forward. The gale whipped through the broken windows and fanned the flames until their crackling and popping arose to a roar. The whole roof was aflame, and long trails of sparks swirled out on the skirts of the gale until they became lost in the driving snow and the night.

In such wise were things when Blanton, the master mechanic, arrived. He had gone home at five o'clock, and it had taken him some time to return from the far side of Rawlings.

The Rawlings volunteer fire department also had appeared on the scene. They could do little. Their machine was stalled in the drifts on the outskirts of the yards and there was no way to get it across the maze of tracks that surrounded the shop buildings. But they began to bring their hose and do what they could.

Blanton, with Kent, came up beside Shadow and surveyed the burning interior of the building. Blanton shook his head.

"It can't be put out," he said to Kent. "About all that we can do is see that it doesn't spread to any of the other buildings. The roof is on fire and a lot of sparks will soon be flying."

Kent nodded. "We'd better get the two lines of hose playing on the roof."

"That's best," Blanton agreed.

He turned and then stopped as a little man elbowed his way hurriedly through the onlookers and stepped up to him. It was Jones, the head storekeeper, and he was plainly excited. He pointed into the machine shop.

"The door . . ."—he asked Blanton—"was the fire door to the oil room closed?"

"Did you leave it open?" Blanton demanded.

Jones gulped. "Part way," he admitted. "I meant to return and didn't bother to close it all the way. Something else came up and I went home and forgot about it until I saw the machine shop was on fire."

Blanton clutched Kent by the arm. "Was the fire door to the oil room shut after four o'clock?" he demanded.

"Fire door?" Kent started and his face paled.

"Yes, fire door! The storekeeper says it was open part way when he left at four o'clock."

Kent shook his head. "I wasn't near it, and I don't think anyone else was, either."

The storekeeper turned a frightened glance on the burning interior. "There were five boxes of dynamite put in there day before yesterday for the construction gang! And a couple of boxes of caps with them!" he shrilled. "And the whole room is stacked with drums of kerosene and paint and oil! There's a lot of box packing there! It's liable to blow up any minute!" He gave another look at the fire and turned and scuttled away.

Shadow and the two men who were helping him hold the nozzle heard the excited declaration of the storekeeper. The man across from Shadow, the machinist who had complained about the heat, paled.

"Didja hear that?" he asked hoarsely.

Shadow nodded and swerved the stream of water over to that part of the rear wall where the fire door was located.

"Looks like we got to keep plenty of water where that door is," he answered coolly.

"Plenty of water," the machinist snorted. "I'm going to put plenty of space between me and the whole dern' building."

He let go of the nozzle and emulated the example of the storekeeper. His companion, without saying a word, followed him.

Shadow wrestled with the squirming hose and swore mightily. "Yellow!" he bawled to the world in general. "Everybody's yellow! C'mere, damn it! Give me a lift!"

The man he shouted at was Blanton, who was nearest him.

Blanton heard him, looked, recognized him and, seeing the situation, sprang from Kent's side and grasped the handle of the nozzle. Kent joined him.

Neither Blanton nor Kent made any reference to Shadow's incongruous actions. Blanton peered into the fire again, and then looked at Kent and at Shadow.

"That door's got to be closed," he stated grimly.

Kent shook his head. "It's too late now. There isn't an opening in the oil room, except some slits along the top of the wall for ventilation. The only way to reach the door is through the shop here. It can't be done now."

Blanton set his jaw. "I think I can get to it," he said. "It isn't very far to the door. Most of the fire is at the ends. Right through the middle here it's just smoke."

"You'll never make it," insisted Kent. "Why, we can't even see halfway to the back wall through the smoke. We'd better warn everyone to get out of the way. It's liable to blow up any minute."

"I'm going to try," declared Blanton stubbornly. "If that room blows up, it will damage the coal tipple and the roundhouse. Our main line service will be interrupted. We can't have that. If I can close that fire door, the machine shop will burn out harmlessly."

Before Kent could remonstrate further, Blanton stripped off his heavy overcoat, wet it in the stream of water, and, holding it before him, plunged into the burning building.

"It's suicide!" Kent cried almost tearfully. "The man's crazy! He'll never get out alive."

Shadow gave him a sour glance. "It's murder to wet a man on a night like this," he observed. "Why shouldn't he try to shut the door? He'll save the company lots of money if he does."

"The company? What's the company beside a man's life?" demanded Kent excitedly.

Shadow squinted into the burning interior. "Shut up," he ordered gruffly. "We gotta keep some water about where he is. He'll make it if we keep him wet."

He raked the stream over the area between the entrance and the place where the fire door was located. But though Shadow spoke confidently, Kent's words soon began to bear the stamp of truth. Blanton should have made the trip in a minute, two minutes at most. One minute, two minutes, three minutes they stood gazing intently into the smoke, watching for Blanton to reappear.

Kent shook his head. "He's never coming back," he said despairingly. "He's somewhere in there burning up right now. I said it was suicide."

"Shut up that blubbering!" snapped Shadow savagely.

He looked around. They were alone. The news that the building might blow up any minute had spread and everyone had retired to a safe distance. The men on the other hose line had pulled it back with them until the stream barely reached the walls of the machine shop.

Shadow's lip curled and his faded blue eyes squinted in contempt. "Yellow!" he grated. "Everyone afraid of his skin. They wouldn't lift a finger for the company that keeps 'em alive."

"Burning," muttered Kent, and his voice barely carried over the crackling of the fire.

Shadow shivered, but it was from the cold gale playing over his wet form, not from fright. He felt strangely light-headed. Kent seemed to have receded a trifle, and, when Shadow glared at him, he seemed to quiver as a shadow does on moving curtains. "Well," said Shadow loudly, "if he's burning, we'll go in and get him and pull him out!"

"You're crazy!" cried Kent. "We'll wait another minute and then we'll get back from here. He was told not to go in. We've done all we can."

"Have we?" asked Shadow, and his throat felt dry and he could hardly speak.

"Yes," insisted Kent. "Come on, let's go back."

He pulled at the nozzle.

"No!" said Shadow, jerking at it.

He shivered and, in the next instant, was burning with heat.

"Come on," said Kent roughly. He pulled at the hose harder.

"No!" said Shadow, and his voice broke and rose to a scream as his self-control snapped. "Damn you! If you're afraid, get out! I'm going in and get him and close that door!"

He let loose of the nozzle and, without stopping to see what Kent did with it, took a deep breath and plunged into the billowing clouds of smoke and heat that swirled out of the door.

It was hot inside, hot as a great oven. Shadow felt as if he were burning up, outside and inside. His eyes were irritated by the smoke and so filled with tears that they were useless. He rubbed at them with the back of his hand, held onto the breath of pure air he had taken outside, and pressed ahead.

The machine shop was over 100 feet deep—100 feet of heat, of smoke, of sparks and embers from overhead, 100 feet of hell. A blazing ember from the burning roof dropped on the back of Shadow's outstretched hand. It seared deeply before he shook it off. Another struck his sleeve and only the wetting Kent had given him saved him from catching afire.

Suddenly his outstretched hand touched something hard and hot, but not the brick of the rear wall. It was a great driving wheel lathe. He remembered it as resting to the left of the oil-room door and some twenty feet in front of it.

His need for another breath became imperative. His heart pounded. His lungs were red hot, bursting. He could stand it no longer. He exhaled with a whistling rush. Then real torture began. What he gulped into his empty lungs was not air. Rather fiery gas, biting smoke. He coughed, choked, gulped again, and doggedly held to the right for four paces. That, he reckoned, put him almost straight in front of the fire door.

Blanton must be found. He had seen nothing of the master mechanic. But he might have passed within three feet of the man and not seen him. Blanton might be burning, even as Kent had said. The oil-soaked floor was blazing in many spots.

But the fire door came first. With it opened only a heavy wire door remained between the contents of the oil room and the fire. One-inch mesh was that wire, nothing at all to keep out the drifting sparks, the licking flames that crept nearer and nearer. Yes, close the door and then look for Blanton. Small satisfaction in searching for him and then getting blasted out of life after he was found.

Thinking so, Shadow held straight ahead with a rush. His foot stubbed into something soft. He tripped and sprawled over an inert body. It was Blanton, slumped, twisted, dead—perhaps.

Shadow, as he groped to his knees, blinded by the smoke, found that which had felled Blanton. It was a heavy block, part of a block and fall that had been suspended above and in front of the oil-room door to load and unload drums of oil from the hand trucks on which they were transported from the loading platform at the end of the building.

The rope with which the top block had been secured had been reached by the fire. It had burned through and the block had dropped on Blanton's head. Shadow's fingers were burned by the smoldering rope ends on the block even as he felt of it.

Dead. Blanton was dead. They would both be dead soon. Shadow's lungs burned, tightened. He felt weak, helpless, slipping. Air. If he could have one breath of pure air! As he knelt to feel of Blanton's heart, he found life for them both.

Blanton's heart beat—slowly, but he lived. Along the floor flowed a current of breathable air. Shadow drew it into his tortured lungs. It gave him new life and courage. He thought of the door. It must be near. Leaving Blanton for the moment, he stood up and went forward.

Within three paces he reached the back wall. It was brick he touched, and he needed the door, the wire door. He felt to the left, found nothing, and, following a sudden conviction, lunged to the right. His scorched fingers touched wire—painfully hot wire. And to the right still farther he found the handle of the fire door. He pulled and the door moved.

Before he closed the fire door tightly, Shadow peered into the oil room for signs of fire. He saw nothing. The drifting sparks had not found their mark as yet. With a heave he closed the door and latched it.

Safe. There would be no explosion on the D&R that night. Kent had said it couldn't be done. It had. But there was Blanton, and the journey back to the entrance of the burning building. The sparks were raining down faster. The *crackling* of the fire was getting louder. The heat of the blazes closing in from both ends of the building was more intense.

Shadow turned back and found Blanton. The master mechanic still lay inert. He was burning, even as Kent had said. His clothes smoldered in a dozen places from the falling embers. Shadow beat at them with his hands. But the cloth was hard to put out and he made little progress. He gave it up. They would have to reach the outside quickly or they would never get there.

He put his face close to the floor and gulped the air again and again. A final deep breath and he got to his feet and grasped Blanton by the shoulders.

Blanton was large and heavy. Shadow was tall and slim and slight. The huge master mechanic was a heavy burden for him at any time. Weakened as Shadow was, it was almost too much for him. He strained and lifted and pulled. Blanton's body stirred, moved, and dragged along the floor. Thus they made the front entrance. Not in one grand rush. Not in one final sweep to victory. Rather in small stretches, with intervals for Shadow to get life from near the floor, with spaces for Shadow to beat at the rain of embers that was falling faster on both of them.

Once a creeping stream of flame barred their progress. Shadow had to pull mightily to get Blanton through before his clothes caught fire in earnest. Once there was an ominous *crackling* from overhead. Shadow's heart sank, for it seemed apparent that the roof was caving in. But he held on. A draft of cold air struck him. A blast of icy water beat upon his back. Pulling Blanton after him, he staggered backward into the open, and the fury of the gale enfolded them with an icy mantle.

Then there was no lack of men to run forward, to congratulate Shadow, to drag them back from the building as the roof caved in with a mighty crash and a shower of sparks and flame, to

carry Blanton to his warm office, to catch Shadow Macgillicuddy as he fainted, to call a doctor for them both.

Days later Shadow came back from the spaces where he had
wandered, weak, delirious, unconscious, a visitor at the
borderline of life and death. Pneumonia had claimed him, and
his thin, scrawny frame had offered little resistance. He was a
true shadow, a human shadow when he opened his sunken,
faded blue eyes and gazed sanely upon the world.

He was in a strange world, a quiet world—quiet and dim and
peaceful. Yes, peaceful and restful, but strange. The wallpaper
on the ceiling and side walls was strange, the pictures on the
wall, the bed, even the quiet and peacefulness were strange.
There never was much quiet where the twelve Macgillicuddy
children lived.

The sound of a distant chime whistle floated into the room,
and a lump came into Shadow's throat. He was near the
railroad, near home—home and his twelve children and their
mother. Twelve children and their mother, and jobless. He was
jobless, he knew. No need to speculate about that. Gatz would
not hold the job open for a day. How long he had been away he
did not know. It was long enough to lose the job. He sensed
that.

Shadow closed his eyes and lay quietly for some time. Finally
hot tears oozed out from between his closed lids. Fourteen
mouths to feed, and he had no job. They were probably hungry.
The tears came faster.

Of a sudden a gruff voice beside him asked: "What's the matter with you now?"

Shadow turned his head and opened his eyes. Leaning in a
doorway, close to the bed, was Blanton, a wan Blanton, a Blanton with his head all wrapped in bandages. Blanton looked at
Shadow sternly.

Somehow, in a way, it seemed natural for Blanton to be there. Shadow looked at him in silence. Finally he asked: "Where am I?"

"My house," said Blanton gruffly. "There wasn't room at your house for a sick man, so they brought you here. Anything else you want to know?"

There was.

"Gatz," said Shadow heavily, "I suppose he's fired me?"

"Yes," said Blanton. "I told him to."

Shadow swallowed. "My kids," he said painfully. "They'll starve. Gatz was the only man with work."

"Bosh," said Blanton roughly. "What do you care about that piddling job? You've got a good job on the railroad. Now that you've got a yard engine to run you ought to be satisfied." He added somewhat unnecessarily: "Ryan was in this morning to see how you are. He comes around almost every day to ask about you."

Shadow's thin hands clenched under the covers, and he swallowed again. The tears came again in spite of himself. "It's a good world," he said, and choked and managed to grin.

Blanton's eyes crinkled and moistened and he nodded.

"It is a good world," he agreed. "A great world if you make it so."

* * * * *

THE TRAIL TO MONTEREY

* * * * *

By 1944, T. T. Flynn was writing fiction primarily for the Popular Publications magazine group, *Argosy*, which by then had become a slick monthly, his Mr. Maddox racetrack mysteries for *Dime Detective*, and Western stories that, depending on length, appeared either in *Dime Western* or *Fifteen Western Tales*. Because Mike Tilden, who edited *Dime Western*, changed virtually all the titles of the stories in each issue according to his own calculus as to what would most appeal to readers, Flynn stopped giving his Western stories titles, leaving this up to the editor. In his story log he placed in parentheses after the word Western (Mex War) for this story. It was accepted on October 18, 1944 and appeared under the title "Guns of the Lobo Trail" in the May, 1945 issue of *Fifteen Western Tales*. The author was paid $225.00.

I

The three riders moved single file and quietly through the thorn brush. Old Tucker Mossby led the way, his wild black beard slightly thrust forward, as if the beard, too, were as alert as Tucker's keen eyes.

John Brent rode second, and Shorty Quade brought up the rear. There was still fire in the setting sun, and heat in these south Texas thorn thickets that slapped a moist grip around a mountain man's throat and brought sweat from every pore.

Brent thought of the beaver country in the high Rockies, 1,000 miles and more behind them, and turned in the saddle with a faint smile.

"Shorty, what'd you give for a mountain camp tonight?"

"Tucker's whiskers an' this whole dern' Mexican War we're tryin' to find," Shorty groaned wistfully. "When I think what you an' Tucker talked me into, I could sit down an' cry. All these weeks of ridin', gettin' shot at by hostile Injuns, an' we find a low-down, thorned-up, god-fersaken country like this. Nary a mountain. Nary a cold spring. If old Gin'ral Taylor's fightin' Mexico over thorny brush like this, he oughta get whupped. I always knowed Texans was queer. They'd have to be to put up with this."

"Quiet!" Tucker Mossby's warning growl reached back to them.

The old mountain hunter had flung his face up and was sniffing, watching the gently moving leaves at the top of an oak,

157

ahead and to the left of the trail.

A moment later Tucker pointed. Not far beyond the tree broad buzzard wings circled low across a patch of sky and went out of sight behind the rampart of thorn brush that sided the trail. Tucker Mossby rode on silently, his greasy, fringed buckskin hunting shirt dark with perspiration.

A few moments later Brent caught the sweet, sickening odor of death, faint, far away, yet noted by old Tucker's nostrils as surely as a wolf ever nosed a hot deer trail.

Wild cattle, unshod horses had traveled the brush trail they were following. None of the sign was fresh, not even the sign they had been following for a day and a half. Tucker's judgment had been as good as any.

"Comanche bucks raidin' toward the Río Grande," Tucker said. "Eight of them, I make it. Might as well let 'em lead us to the river. They'll know the quick way an' the water holes."

The trail swung left. Tucker presently pointed to more buzzards soaring in the rays of the setting sun. Beside the trail in a little grassy clearing a small log cabin stood with its door open invitingly.

The smell of death was stronger. Fresh white bones gleamed in the wild grass near the cabin. Two buzzards took off from the ground with a clumsy rush and beating of wings. Tucker spoke briefly as Brent and Shorty ranged up beside him and they rode toward the cabin.

"Them Comanches got blood here. I bet it was so easy they laughed."

Two horses had been killed. The bones of a man were nearby in the grass, skull grinning toward the blue sky and all bones cleaned by the buzzards.

Shorty picked up a crude leather sandal near the skeleton. "Mexican," he guessed.

Brent walked to the cabin doorway, a tall, powerful, loose-limbed figure, flat-crowned black hat pushed back on his dark damp hair. Since leaving the Ohio River country six years ago he had seen violence and death. He had fought Indians and trapped and traded in the New Mexican settlements. He had become tough and crafty and trail-wise. But he swore at what he found in the ransacked little cabin.

Tucker Mossby stepped in silently as usual. Tucker seemed to melt and flow, to appear and disappear without warning. Now Tucker looked briefly at what was left of the bodies on the hard-packed dirt floor. Two babies, two children not much larger, two women, one of whom had had snowy hair.

"I've knowed good Injuns," Tucker said, and he spat. "They wasn't Comanches." Tucker turned out. "There's a well in back. Might as well camp here. You'll git used to the smell."

There was a well sweep and a crude wooden bucket that brought up sweet fresh water. Brent drank deeply and Shorty followed him, balancing the bucket on the log well curb. Tucker Mossby had moved carelessly around the well with silent steps. His growl came out of the wild black beard.

"Git the hosses here to the well an' water 'em like you wasn't thinkin' of nothin' else. But git your guns ready."

"Trouble?" Brent asked.

"Water's' been spilt on this side. We ain't the first that's drunk here in the last half hour."

Tucker was sitting on the well curb, lazily looking around the grassy opening when Brent and Shorty brought the horses. They had rawhide saddle pockets and blankets strapped behind the saddles. That was all. Pack horses, trail gear had long been lost in running Indian fights far back in the buffalo wilderness.

"They're watchin' us," Tucker grumbled. "Waitin' to see if we make camp or ride on. Injuns again. Bet it's the same bunch that come through here the other day. You can bet they remembered this water. I got one sighted over there in the brush. He's so dern' sure we're easy meat he's bobbin' his head up an' down like a razzled prairie dog."

"I see him," Brent said. "Shorty, it'd be a shame to lose your hair after coming this far."

"Be worse to lose my horse an' have to walk to the Río Grande," Shorty said gloomily. "Tucker, we gonna run?"

A turkey called back in the brush. Another answered nearer the trail and a little farther away. Tucker stood up lazily, his Pennsylvania rifle across a bent arm.

"Draw one more bucket an' I'll tell you. That gobble down the trail sounds like they're set to pick us off if we ride on. An' they'll git us afore dark if we set here." Tucker spat. His wild black beard had a threatening look. "Four little kids," he said. "An' a old gran'maw. I mean to git me that red-hided prairie dog over there while I got the light. I'll bet he's the one that kilt ol' gran'maw."

The last horse drank the last bucket of water dry. Turkey calls drifted through the thorn brush.

"Jump on the horses quick when I shoot him," Tucker said. "Ride to the other side of the clearing an' sort of circle fast to draw some shots. My guess is there won't be none on that side."

"Why not ride into the brush over there and see if they follow?" Brent suggested. "Might catch them out in the open if they get the idea we're leaving fast."

"You always come up with a good idee," Tucker granted. He spat again. "I had the same idee. You ready?"

No one answered. They rode and fought and worked this way, three men used to each other, trusting each other, usually thinking alike. Tucker Mossby was the best shot. He could take the eye out of a sitting jack rabbit almost as far as the small animal was visible. Tucker stepped to his horse as if to mount, and aimed and fired with one smooth quick motion.

Brent glimpsed a quick flurry of motion where the Indian had been watching. By the time he forked the saddle the sound of the shot was followed by silence.

"Got him in the head!" Tucker exclaimed. "Now he can tell gran'maw how it feels!"

A high-pitched howl of warning rang from the brush. Gunshots broke raggedly after them. Tucker Mossby yelled as they circled in the clearing at full gallop.

"Only four guns so far! It's that small bunch of Comanch'! Bust back in the brush after 'em afore the devils git a chance to reload!" Tucker set the example by howling wildy and charging the brush. Brent and Shorty followed, spreading out. They could fight this way, changing plans, each knowing what to do. They struck the brush, leaning low forward, and knowing that the thorns would rip and tear.

Beyond whipping branches, Brent sighted a darting shadow off to the left. He reined sharply that way, lost the figure, and then got a quick sight of a bare, dodging torso. The man wheeled, fired a heavy musket, missed. Thorns slashed Brent's face. He held steady and fired the Colt revolver he carried and preferred. He saw the brown figure plunge down, try to scramble up, and fall flat again.

Blood was oozing on Brent's face as he reined to a stop beside the dark-skinned figure. He heard two fast shots over toward the trail, and the farther battle whoop of Tucker Mossby and the plunging rush of Tucker's horse. But as the man he had shot rolled over and showed a hideously painted face in black, red, white stripes, Brent swung fast out of the saddle. The man was dying, red froth on his lips, eyes rolling, chest heaving as he tried to breathe. Brent roughly ran fingers through the man's light brown hair, and wet a fingertip and rubbed a spot on the bony chest. The brownish-red color lightened and showed dingy white skin where he rubbed.

163

"Thought so," Brent said. "White man, aren't you?"

The rolling eyes fixed on him. The man stopped struggling for breath, as if in the haze of death he were trying to collect himself, to think.

"How many more like you around here?" Brent asked.

The man sucked a convulsive, bubbling breath. His fists clenched, the cords in his brown throat tightened as he gasped: "Polly dancing Matamoras. Watch rooster."

"What's that?" Brent demanded, bending lower.

But he was speaking to a dying man, whose life gushed from a slack and silent mouth.

Frowning, Brent stood up. He heard another burst of shots, and he rode through the thorn brush in that direction. When he sighted another dodging figure, he held fire and spurred after it.

He was riding down a slender youth, dressed in shirt, pants, and armed only with a hunting knife. He could have killed the fugitive, but he rode the youth down instead, and made a flying drop from the saddle, revolver in one hand, rifle in the other. He was met with a rush and the slashing knife.

Brent was head and shoulders taller. There was something so laughable about the sobbing fury of the attack that Brent dropped both guns and met the rush, grinning and empty-handed. Even at that he was surprised at the ease with which he slapped the knife aside, and then wrenched it from a small, brown-stained hand. For this was another white one, with fine dark hair tied back with a red cloth about the forehead.

"Hold quiet, you young snake," Brent panted. "White or red, I oughta kill you, and maybe I will." He slapped the scuffling figure reeling.

"¡Madre de Dios! You slap me?" was the furiously sobbing threat that came with another rush.

Brent caught at a hand that was trying to rake fingernails across his face. He missed the hand and got the shirt instead,

162

and the power of his grip tore the old sleeve half off. "You ain't a man!" Brent gulped, backing away.

Breathing hard, tears of rage and fright still on her stained cheeks, she stood holding the torn shirt together. Now Brent saw that the fine brown hair, cut long for a boy but short for a girl, was trying to curl under the edges of the red head cloth. She could not be twenty. He guessed eighteen, small, with a boyish build. She had made a handsome youth. She made a prettier girl, and the dark-tinted skin of her face and neck and hands did her no harm. Under the torn shirt her arm had been whiter than Brent's.

She watched silently as Brent picked up his guns. He had shoved her knife inside his belt.

"What's your name?" Brent questioned. She looked back silently.

A rider approached through the brush. Brent stepped to his horse and waited warily. The girl gave an uneasy look toward the approaching sounds and edged toward him, still holding the shirt together with one hand.

Tucker Mossby yelled: "Johnny Brent!"

"Here!"

"Got him, did you?" Tucker remarked with satisfaction as he rode up. "I kilt a couple back there where their hoses was tied. Four of them was tryin' to get mounted. One big buck was draggin' this 'n' onto a hoss with him. But when I cut loose, this 'n' fell off an' the big feller sold out alone. This 'n' run off. I'll swear the big 'n' had red hair. Mean-lookin'. You gonna shoot this 'n, or you want me to?"

"Did you look close at the ones you killed?"

"Hell's fire! When I'm killin' Injuns, I ain't got time to look!"

"Go back and look. I'll take care of this one."

"Shoot him in the back fer ol' gran'maw an' her white hair," Tucker advised callously.

"How many in your party?" Brent asked the girl when Tucker rode off.

"Eight." She sniffed and stole a look at him.

"Eight thieving, killing renegades! You heard him tell me to kill you."

She nodded, biting her lip.

"Colored like an Indian! Killing babies and old women!"

The girl nodded. "*Sí, señor*, if you say so. How many babies?"

"Four," said Bent, getting angry.

"*Sí, señor.* Four if you say so."

"Do you know what I'm talking about?"

"No, *señor*."

"Don't call me that. You can talk good English."

She smiled faintly and said nothing.

"What's your name?"

The red tip of her small tongue paused between her lips thoughtfully. "Rosita," she decided.

"That's not your right name!"

She smiled faintly again and watched him.

"Who's Polly?"

She stiffened ever so slightly. Johnny Brent thought fright appeared in her look. He was not sure. All the expression faded out of her face. She had lost her fear of him. She had edged instinctively toward him for safety when Tucker Mossby rode up. Now that feeling was gone. She stood with sober watchfulness, like a trapped and waiting wild thing.

"Keep close to me," Brent warned, leading his horse in the direction Tucker had vanished.

Rosita walked beside him. Once she stepped quickly forward and held up a low-hanging thorn branch. Brent grunted thanks. She did not look at him.

Shorty and Tucker Mossby were in a small grassy opening. Two pack horses and three saddled horses were still tied there.

Tucker was swearing.

"Renegades. An' I thought they was Injuns. Hell. They're wuss'n Comanch'. Whyn't you kill that young devil? Git away from him, Johnny, an' I'll shoot him. I ain't even waitin' to ask him questions." Tucker cocked his revolver and loosed a string of lurid and threatening profanity.

Rosita dodged behind Brent. He could feel her hand tremble as she clutched his shirt.

"Hold it, Tucker! You don't want to kill a girl, do you?"

"What's that?" Tucker roared. He stared, open-mouthed, and lowered the gun and stalked closer. Rosita shrank closer against Brent. "I'll be. . . ." Tucker swallowed. "I'll be . . . ," he said again weakly.

Shorty had come from the pack horses, and now Shorty's weathered and sharp face puckered in quick admiration. "Purty, ain't she?"

Tucker holstered his gun and snorted. "Prob'ly she's the one kilt old gran'maw. Nothin' beats a squaw for bein' blood-thirsty when she gets a chance."

Rosita stiffened inside Brent's arms and flared angrily: "Don't you call me a squaw!"

"White girl," Tucker muttered. "Mean-tempered, too." He gave Brent a reproachful look. "Long as you didn't kill her, you got to worry with her. Better find out what kind of a snake's nest we busted up here."

"Her name is Rosita, and she won't talk," Brent said.

"Whup her," Tucker advised. "I had me a Blackfoot squaw who got contrary an' plagued me until I snatched a willow switch an' whupped her twicet around the teepee. You never seen a woman git so sweet. She tole me later it proved I wanted to keep her."

"I might try it." Brent chuckled.

"First you better look in them packs," Shorty said. "They got some U.S. Army uniforms. Tucker, you an' your Comanches. Maybe we've shot up Gin'ral Taylor's army. Hell of a note after comin' all this way to help out."

"When I see a red face painted an' skulkin' close, I start talkin' after the shootin'," Tucker growled. "Lemme look at them packs. Brent, find out from the girl."

She had moved away from Brent and was looking at him with close attention. Now she cast a glance of dislike after Tucker Mossby and waited until he was out of earshot.

"Please, *señor*. Of this I know nothing. I was a prisoner. See."

Rosita held out her hands, and now Brent noticed red chafe marks at her wrists where ropes had been tied tightly.

"How long were you with them?"

"Two days. I theenk they are Indians when they come to my camp. They keel my *mozo*."

"Where were you going?"

"To see my old nurse."

"Where does she live?"

Rosita shrugged. "*Mi mozo*, he tak' me. I don' know where we go."

"Where did you come from?"

"Matamoras," said Rosita after a moment's hesitation.

"Get on one of those horses and come with me," Brent said grimly.

Rosita obeyed silently. Brent told Tucker and Shorty they'd be back quickly, and a little later he ordered Rosita to dismount at the gaping doorway of the cabin.

She looked, wide-eyed, at the bones out in the grass, and a gasp escaped her when they walked inside.

"This mean anything to you?" Brent asked coldly.

She was frozen and quiet as she walked about what was left of the bodies. She bent over the old woman's white hair and crossed herself. While Brent watched her without emotion, she stooped and touched one tiny, little blue cloth boot that had been on a baby's foot. A whimper escaped her, and she suddenly bolted outside.

He saw sobs shaking her as she ran to her horse. Brent followed more leisurely. She dashed tears from her eyes with the back of her hand. And then, handling the horse as only an expert rider could, she wheeled past the head of Brent's horse, snatched the reins with a lithe downsweep of her body, and bolted toward the trail, leading his horse.

"Come back here!" Brent shouted.

He lifted the rifle. There was still enough light to aim. He could have dropped her small figure from the saddle with one careful shot. But Brent knew he wouldn't.

He was angry and puzzled and helpless afoot as he watched her ride out of sight, and yet he held fire and let her go and started back afoot to face Tucker and Shorty.

"She threw a spell on you," Shorty said with sly generosity. "Bet she'd 'a' done the same thing to me. Now wasn't she a purty gal, though? Enough to make a feller stand around with moon eyes an' no sense left in his haid?"

"You ain't learnt how to handle women," Tucker growled. "I seen her sizin' you up. Knowed she was set to hand you a trick, but I figgered you're old enough to start larnin'. Johnny, this bunch was renegade soldiers outta Taylor's army, or they been stealin' or killin' around the army. They ain't Mexicans. They're white men, an' it don't make sense."

"We might find out in Matamoras," Brent said. "Going to camp here tonight?"

"Why not?" Tucker grumbled. "We got to rest the hosses, an' we might get a live visitor we can holt onto an' question." Tucker spat. "If it's another woman, I'll handle her."

II

Two days later they rode off the scow ferry into Matamoras, near the mouth of the Río Grande, and found the town a wild eddy of heat and dust and war in this summer of 1845. Taylor had won his battles of Palo Alto and Resaca de la Palma. His Pittsburgh-built riverboats were running supplies up the river to the new base at Camargo. That night Brent, Tucker, and Shorty wandered around town and watched hell's broth boiling.

The twelve-months volunteers off the troop transports at Brazos de Santiago anchorage were running wild. Tequila, *pulque,* aguardiente, and raw Monogahela whiskey from the States were being guzzled on every side.

Brent watched with disgust as drunken privates whooped at passing officers. Grog shops were crowded; fandangos were bedlams of raucous music, bawdy songs, wild voices, furious fights. Gambling games were running everywhere.

"Well, we heerd they was fightin' on the Río Grande," Short said. "Nobody said it was likker they was fightin'."

Tucker Mossby had stalked the streets with his silent tread, all expression hidden by his ragged black beard. He was a strange and rather savage sight in his greasy leather hunting shirt and wide-brimmed felt hat.

"Might as well git back to the corral," Tucker said. "Tomorrow we can turn them Army uniforms over an' jine up. From the looks of this town ol' Taylor needs us." Tucker spat. "I ain't surprised now at anything we run onto back there in the brush. Git some of these rascals out on the loose an' they'd try anything."

"Let's look into another *cantina* or two," Brent suggested. "Here's one ahead that's more lively than any we've seen."

All evening it had been this way, Brent leading them into the noisiest spots. They had had two drinks and let it go at that. In each place Brent had looked around and found his chance to ask quietly for a dancer named Polly. He had not told Tucker and Shorty about that. He had said little about the girl who called herself Rosita. But she had been on his mind, and he had kept thinking of the dying man, who had said Polly was dancing in Matamoras, and a rooster must be watched. He kept thinking of the bodies back in the lonely little clearing, and the tears Rosita had dashed from her eyes as she rode recklessly away from the muzzle of his gun.

Brent led the way into the noisy crowd that filled the wide, low-ceilinged adobe building. Tucker's powerful hand closed on his arm.

"Look!" Tucker said, pointing with his chin and black beard. "What devil turned her into an angel an' put her dancin' here?"

In the reeking haze of lamplight and tobacco smoke a girl was dancing on a raised platform at the end of the long room. Two squeaking fiddles, a guitar, and a small thumped drum made fast and wild music that was muted by the clamorous crowd.

The girl did not seem to mind. She might have had a fine orchestra at her feet and magic music in her heels and toes. One forgot her shabby black dress and the solid pink shawl of fringed silk she deftly handled. The delicacy of her features, the fire of her movements held Brent.

She had now a dancer's graceful slenderness, and her short hair was a curly halo about her head, and her small hands were incredibly expressive. Tonight before this drunken riff-raff she was like fine champagne, fired with life, with promise.

Brent had to look twice to make sure he was seeing right over the heads of the crowd. And then he was sure of it, as Tucker had been at first sight. The dancer was Rosita, the brown tint covering all her bare arms now, and the boyish side of her lost in this exciting, graceful girl.

Brent began to push through the crowd toward her. Dark,

ragged Mexicans were making the music. They looked brutish and sullen in contrast to the gay girl dancing on the platform.

"*Yo amo*," Rosita sang in clear Spanish, "I love, love. . . ."

Most of the volunteers were ignorant of the language. A few civilians in the place—scouts, teamsters, sutlers—understood. Encouraging yells came from several of them.

A big, rough-bearded man shouted: "I'm the rooster ye're lookin' to love, purty gal! Here I come!" He leaped on the platform and caught her arm.

Rosita lost step and tried to pull away. The stranger whooped, pulled her toward him, and Brent broke through the last watchers and jumped up on the platform, also.

The fiddles were still sawing and the drum was sounding lamely as Brent dropped a hand on the man's arm and said coldly: "The lady was waiting for me."

Rosita's eyes went wide with astonishment as she recognized Brent. In good English she panted: "He has many friends here."

The stranger wheeled on Brent. Rosita twisted away as he released her.

"Fust come gits her, you fool!"

A big fist struck fast and hard while the man was still speaking; it hit Brent's cheek and rocked him. It hurt.

But Brent was grinning with a quick and savage surge of released tension as he smashed the man's bearded face in a fast return. He hit with trail-hard, corded muscles that drove the big stranger reeling.

"Fight fer the slut, will ye?" the man bellowed. He crouched and snatched a Bowie knife from under his coat. "I'll cut you into chunks!"

Tucker Mossby's warning shout rang out: "Look sharp, Johnny! Back down here!"

They had left their guns at the corral, on advice that armed civilians were inviting trouble if they walked among the drunken troops at night. Knives were another matter. Brent had a hunting knife, but he let that stay out of sight and hurled his hat fully in the bearded face. While the big stranger was blinded for an instant, Brent caught he wrist above the Bowie blade.

The man yelled angrily, tried to snatch the knife with the other hand. Brent smashed knuckles to his mouth. The man quivered, stiffened, bellowed wildly, and staggered back, clapping a hand to his side.

Rosita was circling back of him, a small dagger in her brown-stained hand. The stranger turned his bleeding mouth to the crowd and his yell was hoarse.

"Will ye see Ben White knifed dirty? Company A! Yer sutler's knifed from the back!"

Brent thought the girl had stabbed with her dagger. Then the stranger held up a bloody dirk, man-size, deadly. He was staring at it dazedly as an uproar broke out around the platform and spread through the big room.

"Help Ben White! They're killin' Ben White! A Company! C Company! Git our sutler! Tear down this dirty hole!"

An empty whiskey bottle grazed Brent's head. He caught the Bowie knife off the dusty boards where the sutler had dropped it. He turned to find Tucker Mossby standing on the platform edge, slugging at men who were trying to climb up. Shorty was doing the same.

More bottles began to hurtle through the air. Brent jumped to help Tucker, who was kicking at hands trying to seize his legs. A wall lamp was knocked out of its bracket. Another bottle broke one of the ceiling lamps.

Brent felt a hand on his arm. He whirled to slash with the Bowie knife and he met Rosita's breathless voice.

"This way, before they kill you. Quick! The door!"

Once more Brent noticed that she was using English as well as he could speak it. Rosita had thrown the pink silk shawl over the bearded sutler's head. The man was tearing it off and still holding the knife that had stabbed him.

A bottle struck a large brass lamp hanging over the platform. Glass scattered as the light flickered out. Another bottle hit Brent's shoulder with terrific force. In the murky dimness the crowd was turning into a mob of rising temper. Brent caught the faint glint of a bayonet flying toward him, point first. He barely dodged it.

"Quick," Rosita panted, tugging at his arm.

"Get out of here!" Brent told her harshly. He swung around and called: "Tucker, Shorty! This way!"

Rosita waited at the side of the platform until they started toward her. With quick grace she slipped toward a narrow door in the back wall, near the platform.

The last of her shabby orchestra was scuttling out the door. A lanky private tried to cut her off and snatched at her arm. Rosita's smaller dagger threatened him. He looked and saw Brent's Bowie knife and Tucker Mossby's wild black beard coming, and he dived back into the safety of the crowd.

They reached the door and crowded out into the black night. Brent heard Shorty trip over something and swear lustily. A moment later Brent went hard into a solid log wall, and swore himself.

"This way!" Rosita's voice cried behind him. "Here, *señor*, give me your hand! Quick!"

Her small hand groped and clung tightly to his wrist. She pulled him to the left as men boiled out into the darkness after them. Tucker Mossby clapped a hand to Brent's shoulder and followed.

Behind them the pursuit fell over boxes and ran into the log wall. Angry oaths laced the darkness. Brent sensed that he was being led through a low log shed and out a door in the back. Rosita hurried him along a filthy alley where big rats scampered, and they came out into a narrow, winding side street where an occasional curtained window gave out faint light.

"Hurry," Rosita panted.

Tucker Mossby ranged up on the other side of her. "Lady, did you knife that drunken fool?"

Rosita laughed shakily. "Palo, the drummer, threw eet. He ees ver' good with knife."

"Where we going?" Shorty asked.

Tucker answered grimly. "We're gonna go to a quiet spot an' talk with this gal. There's a heap of questions fer her to answer. I aim to ask 'em."

"In here," Rosita said hastily.

She groped at a dark door, opened it, and urged Brent past her into the unlighted interior. Tucker and Shorty followed him, and the door closed.

"This your place, lady?" Tucker demanded.

Rosita did not answer.

"Outside!" Brent blurted. "She's tricked us!"

They had the street to themselves when they bolted out. Shorty laughed under his breath. "Tucker, what was it you aimed to do? Handle her like a squaw?"

"I never seen the beat," Tucker said with grudging admiration. "Let's git back to the corral. I've had enough for one night."

Brent said nothing. But as they groped into one of the wider streets where there was more light and they could ask their way to the corral where they would sleep near the horses, Brent slowly rubbed the wrist Rosita had gripped.

The Brazos corral, newly named and newly owned by a stolid German named Luntz, out of the Texas settlements, was surrounded by wagons and carts and filled with more wagons. Horses, mules were tied around three sides, and the fourth side was a low-roofed shed open in front and bedded with clean dry grass for drivers and riders to sleep on. Luntz held up a smoky lantern at the gate and scanned their faces. "I light you," he mumbled, and led the way with the lantern to the end of the shed where the packs they had brought to Matamoras had been left. "Here," the German said, and he backed off. "I haf your veapons. The shentlemen will shood if you run."

"You men are under military arrest!" a crisp voice said. "Squad, close in!"

"Arrest, hell!" Tucker blurted angrily. "Who's arrestin' me fer what?"

"Tucker! Be careful!" Brent warned sharply.

Tucker had already whirled like a wrathful shadow and knocked down a strange figure that stepped in and caught his arm. But other figures rushed out of the shadows with muskets held ready. Tucker went down fighting under a wave of blue-clad figures, any one of whom might have orders to shoot if resisted.

This obviously was military arrest. Brent held his temper as hands seized him, and appealed to the young officer in charge.

"It's all a mistake. Tell them to hold him until we can talk."

"Orders," said the young lieutenant briefly when they were marched into a dim patio and ordered into a cell-like room, unlighted save by the feeble patio lanterns that showed guards with fixed bayonets slowly pacing.

He was a callow young officer with a blond mustache. He swaggered a little in his brave blue and gold. There was a military snap to his orders and his curtness to prisoners.

"Captain Blandon will see you men in the morning," he said. "All guards have orders to shoot if prisoners try to escape. Corporal, lock them in."

A solid wooden door slammed shut. Orders were snapped outside, and they were alone with a scant barred window high up at the front and another at the back of the room.

"Well, you, jined up, Tucker." Shorty chuckled in the absolute blackness through which they could only grope.

Tucker's lurid opinion lasted for some moments. Then Tucker groaned, swore again. "Ol' Gin'ral Taylor hisself was the onliest one of his army that wasn't piled on me. Johnny, what you make of all this?"

"Might have been that fight tonight in the *cantina*."

"All this fer a fight that wa'nt no shucks, anyways?"

"The sutler was stabbed. He may be dead. If he is, we'll be blamed for it."

"I wonder if Gin'ral Taylor hangs 'em or shoots 'em fer a killing," Shorty mused. "I bet your old neck'll stretch like a tom turkey's, Tucker, when the rope goes tight."

"We'll know in the morning," Brent said. "I'm going to sleep."

In the morning they were given salt meat, coffee, corn pone, a bucket of water to wash in. Tucker looked as usual, save for a slight limp where a musket butt had smashed his leg.

But Brent missed the shave he tried to take each day, and the hard dirt floors of the room, without even a blanket, had not left him any too limber when they were ordered, blinking, into the sun-flooded patio, and marched under guard to a bare-walled room at front.

"How's your neck feel this mornin', Tucker?" Shorty asked as they were ordered into the room.

Tucker snorted. Brent was sober, watchful as he stepped into the room. Chairs, a table near a window, several battered brass spittoons were the furnishings. An Army captain sat at the table, scanning papers, and, when Brent looked at the man, his eyes narrowed watchfully, and yet with some hope.

This young captain had a lean, professional look. His blue uniform was dusty; even his face and brown mustache were dusty, and he sat relaxed as if muscle and bone and spirit were tired. His eyes had a heavy, tired look that steadied into estimating interest as he regarded them.

"Close the door, Sergeant. We'll not be disturbed . . . except on urgent orders." When the closing door left the high-ceilinged, white-walled room quiet and cool, the officer said: "I'm Captain Blandon. Your names, please."

He had pleasant, not unhandsome face beneath the dust and weariness. He wrote their names with a firm, flourishing stroke, and regarded them thoughtfully.

"What're you men doing on the Río Grande?"

"Come to jine up," Tucker grumbled.

"When did you get to Matamoras?"

"Crossed the river when the sun was half down," Tucker answered irritably. "What's all this fer, Cap'n?"

"Did you speak to anyone yesterday about enlisting?"

"Hell, no! We aimed to look around a bit afore some young squirt got a right to order us around."

"Where are you from?"

"T'other side of Pike's Peak, fur as you keer to trap beaver or take chances with your hair."

Captain Blandon's tired eyes lighted with quick interest. He straightened in the chair and put the pen down. "Which way did you come?"

"Down acrost the Llano Estacado an' the buff'ler an' Injun country."

"Why that way?"

"Quickest."

The ghost of a smile warmed Captain Blanford's face at the laconic answer. "Have any trouble along the way?"

"Plenty."

"Kill many Indians?"

"They knowed we passed through."

"Kill anyone else?"

Tucker's mouth was open for reply. He thought better of it, and scowled at the captain and combed the fingers of one hand slowly through his wild black beard. "Who else'd we kill?" Tucker growled after a moment.

"United States Army equipment was found in your packs at the Brazos corral," Captain Blandon said evenly. "Did you bring uniforms from Pike's Peak to wear when you enlisted?"

Tucker opened his mouth again, and again closed it silently. He looked at Brent, who had been watching attentively.

"I think Captain Blandon had better understand fully what happened," Brent said. "As a matter of fact, Captain, it was our intention to inform the proper authorities this morning. Yesterday we'd come a long way without seeing many people. Perhaps you'll understand why we delayed other matters to look around Matamoras."

"I've made a trip or two myself, Mister Brent. But under the circumstances . . . whatever they were . . . we're at war, you know. Recent issue Army uniforms require explaining." The captain cleared his throat. "You're a mountain man, too?"

"In a manner of speaking. I've been told a few more years might make me a fair fur man."

This time the captain's smile was more evident on his tired face. "Explain, Mister Brent, if you please, the uniforms which one of my men found when we examined your packs. We keep an eye on strangers, you see." Captain Blandon leaned back. His fingers touched the ends of his dusty brown mustache; his manner was noncommittal.

Brent explained in detail, to the flight of the girl. He added the discovery of Rosita at the *cantina,* and the way she had vanished again after the fight. "I don't know who the men were we shot. Obviously they meant no good to us. We were justified in shooting, considering other experiences on the trip with Indians. These men made no attempt to break off the trouble.

Is it possible, Captain Blandon, that General Taylor's men are out in the brush masquerading as Indians?"

"Injuns or not, they gits shot when they skulk up on me with war paint!" Tucker Mossby growled. "I ain't never had time to ask no Army gin'ral if his men is out havin' a playful time."

"There is something more," said Brent. He repeated the words of the man he had shot: Polly dancing Matamoras. Watch rooster.

"You kept dern' quiet about that!" Tucker exclaimed. "Bet you was lookin' for that Polly in all them *cantinas* last night."

Captain Blandon was leaning forward. "Was that all the man said?"

"Yes. It meant nothing to me. I was hardly able to understand him. But I think that's what he said."

The captain drummed fingertips lightly on the table.

"The Texas men are doing fine work as scouts," he said. "They know the country. The Mexicans are afraid of them. I know many of them. Fine men, blooded on the frontier for years. But there's other work to be done more softly, quietly than the Rangers like to work. And by its nature more danger-ous at times. I'm detached from my regiment by personal order of General Taylor to command irregulars. I choose who I need." Blandon's smile was almost apologetic in its lack of boast. "You might say my orders are the general's personal orders."

"Christmas," Tucker said softly. Then the glint of interest in Tucker's eyes became stricken. Tucker swallowed. "You didn't send some of your men scoutin' north of the Río in Injun war paint, did you, Cap'n?"

"As a matter of fact I did," Captain Blandon said. He tapped softly with his fingers. "I sent a man named Murphy north of the river. He's lived for years around Saltillo and Monterrey. He admitted joining the San Patricio battalion and then deserting."

"Sounds like a Mex outfit," Shorty observed.

Captain Blandon nodded. "Many of the San Patricios are Irish deserters from our forces. There are other nationalities, too. They're a fine lot of rascals, and Murphy would have been at home with them. He was often called Red Murphy. I'm told the Mexicans called him the Red Rooster."

Tucker slapped his leg. "That big buck who got away had red hair! I'll swear to it. Was this here Rooster a big 'un?"

"Yes." Blandon hunched his tired shoulders. "I seem to have made a mistake. Murphy should have been back days ago. We'll not see him again, I'm afraid."

"What was he doing when we met him?" Brent questioned.

"Some rascality outside of his orders." Blandon drew a breath, dropped his clenched fist softly on the table. "I'm responsible, I suppose, for trusting him. He knows some of my men now, which makes him dangerous. My men don't go in large groups. Murphy can do harm, if he's so minded."

"Perhaps." Brent suggested, "you know something about this dancer. Polly?"

"No. If she's in Matamoras, I'll have her found. Probably she's a sweetheart of Murphy's. He was a great one with the ladies, I've also been told."

"He had a gal with him," Shorty reminded.

"A gal we caught a-dancin' here in Matamoras," Tucker growled.

Brent felt color in his cheeks as they looked at him. "She was no sweetheart of a man like this Murphy," Brent said positively.

"Since you're so sure of it, we'll wait and see," Captain Blandon said, smiling. "Rosita, eh? Did you say she was pretty, Mister Brent?"

"I didn't say," Brent answered. "Tucker's probably a better judge than I am."

"Jes' looked like a woman t' me," said Tucker. "Seen a thousand in my day, all jes' women."

Captain Blandon chuckled. "We'll probably find this Polly, whoever she is, spying for the Mexicans. They're all around us. Hating us for the most part. Can't say I blame them. After all, it's their county. But General Taylor's on his way to take Monterey and get on south into the valley of Mexico and end the war. Are you men still agreeable to enlisting?"

"We came a long way to git us a fight," Tucker said readily.

"Know any Spanish?"

"We all speak it," Brent said. "Santa Fé and the upper Río Grande settlements were in our back yard, you might say. A man had to talk the lingo to get along."

"You're new in these parts. So much the better. Your faces aren't known," Blandon said, as if arguing with himself. He stood up. He was tall and wiry. "I can use men like you. Need you in fact. It's a long way to the valley of Mexico."

"I've been wonderin' who was gonna say it fust," Tucker said, standing up, also. "Cap'n, you got us. What do we do?"

"Find Murphy and bring him in or kill him," said Captain Blandon, gathering up papers. "I don't know what he's up to, and I want him stopped. You'll ride upriver to Camargo, and wait for orders at Rancho Perez, south of the town." Brandon smiled grimly. "After you take the oath, your orders will be military commands, to be obeyed unquestioningly. I'm a regular Army man. I'll have none of this sloppiness you may have observed among the volunteers. The fact that you'll be out of uniform and on regular duty will make no difference, in your strict obedience to orders. Do you understand?"

"I think, sir," said Brent, "we like to hear that kind of talk."

"I ain't tried takin' orders fer a long time," Tucker said. "I reckon I can swaller it."

"Me, too," Shorty assented.

"Then I'll swear you in," said Captain Blandon.

III

Camargo was a flood-ruined and all but deserted town that throbbed with new and alien life as Taylor's army and supplies poured in by land and river. Through chaparral, swampy lowlands, open *llanos*, Brent, Tucker, Shorty made the 100-mile trip in four days, and now and then they sighted the graceful, heavily loaded riverboats pushing against the muddy Río Grande current on the longer water trip.

They passed dragoons and marching infantry and once a battery of field guns trundling heavily on massive, spoked wheels. At Camargo they found vast stacks of supplies along the high riverbanks, and the great plaza of the ruined town seething with soldiers and wagons, pack burros and mules, and the cotton tents of the regiments ranked far outside the town.

Young officers galloped about their business, muleteers cursed luridly, soldiers strolled about or marched past in brisk files, and over all hung dust and heat and the heady feel of action and coming danger. Monterey and the Mexican forces under General *Don* Pedro Ampudia were ahead. Old Zack Taylor knew where he was going and he was on his way.

"This is more like it," Trucker said as they rode out of town in search of Rancho Perez. "Wisht I knowed what we was gonna do."

"Kill us a red-headed rooster," said Shorty cheerfully.

"He didn't say where we'd git the rascal," Tucker grumbled. "Whyn't he let us backtrack to that cabin? Should 'a' stayed home if we couldn't cold track that renegade to where he went."

"Captain Blandon had other ideas. You're under orders now," Brent reminded.

"Wonder if he's got that gal locked up by now. That Rosita," Shorty said gravely, "she'd hang purtier'n a strung yucca flower, wouldn't she? A-kickin' her purty little heels an' her neck a-stretchin' out at the end of the rope."

"No doubt," Brent agreed. Blood crept to his face under Shorty's sly glance.

"Keepin' her to hang'll be the hard thing," Tucker said dryly. "Johnny, you reckon a husband'd have ary chance keepin' her long?" Tucker coughed. "Or mebbe you ain't thought along them lines."

"How could I think of anything with you two fools chattering like piñon jays?" Brent snapped.

Shorty snorted with laughter. Tucker's black beard gave out a dry rumble of humor; even Brent had to grin sheepishly. So they came an hour later, and after one false turn off the rutted dusty road, to Rancho Perez.

Melons, maize, a little wheat were growing on a scant plot of cleared land. A low adobe house had a solid and prosperous look in contrast to the mud-daubed *jacales* of the peons across the clearing.

Horses were in two corrals, Army wagons were standing about, cotton tents were pitched in two rows off to one side, with soldiers loitering among them and muskets stacked in the open. An armed guard was pacing in front of the ranch house.

Brent asked for Lieutenant Fox, as he'd been directed. The man who came out had a young, brisk, cold-eyed look. He read the sealed orders Brent had brought and stared at them curiously.

"You'll find tents over there," he said. "Rations will be issued. The dragoons on duty are a guard and won't pry into your business. If your horses aren't up to hard riding, you can have your pick of better ones."

"That all, sir?" Brent asked.

"Rest while you can. Stay within call. Be ready to leave at any time." The lieutenant regarded their faces. His smile was friendly. "Captain Blandon's men don't put on fat," he answered unspoken questions.

The dragoons looked like a picked lot. They regarded the newcomers without much curiosity, as if used to such visitors, and they asked no questions. They kept to themselves.

Skirmishing parties passed on the road, laughing, singing. Foraging wagons under armed guard creaked by from Camargo and returned. That night Brent was aware of arrivals and departures from the ranch house. A man or two at a time usually. Never large numbers. Two days passed and nothing happened. Tucker began to chafe.

"Reckon we're fergot?"

"Ask the lieutenant," Brent suggested.

Tucker did. He returned to the tents and shrugged. "The lieutenant says Cap'n, Blandon ain't fergetful."

At dusk the captain himself rode in on a lathered, dead-beat horse. He sent for Brent, and talked to him before Lieutenant Fox in the low-roofed front room of the ranch house where oil lamps had already been lighted.

Captain Blandon was dust-covered again. The tired look was heavier on him. He paced slowly about the room, eating cold meat and bread, sipping a glass of wine as he talked.

"You men will leave at dark. Full dark. Three days' rations. Extra rounds for your revolvers and rifles." The captain took another bite of bread and meat and washed it down with a gulp of wine. "I'm glad to see you're all armed with the new Texas revolvers. Wonderful guns. Sam Walker did more than he knew when he went East and got Colt to design that gun."

Brent nodded. "The traders brought a few of them into the mountains. We paid high, and found them worth it."

"You can depend on your horses?"

"We picked new ones, sir."

"Including that black stallion you fancied, Captain," said Lieutenant Fox humorously. "I'll swear I thought three Yankee traders had been turned loose on us, the way they culled the corral and took out the three best."

Captain Blandon chuckled. "Some Mexican *don* is gnashing his teeth over losing that black. No *ranchería* in the chaparral ever had a horse like that black."

"If the captain would rather have him . . . ," Brent suggested.

"No, no. I'm pleased to see such a good eye for horseflesh. Now, then, Brent, you men will ride quietly after full dark, and at the Well of the Ten Crosses and Jesus, halfway between here and Camargo, a rider will be waiting for you, or will be along shortly. You know the place?"

"We spoke of it as we passed this way, sir."

"Good. The password will be *canales*. The answer *muerte*. After that you men will follow orders." The captain cleared his throat. His smile had a certain grim humor. "You will not question the orders. Do you want to ask anything now?"

"Well, no, sir."

"Good luck then, Brent. To all of you."

The captain still had the grim smile of humor as Brent walked out. Tucker and Shorty were elated. Darkness without moon was around them as they rode out quietly in the flour-like road dust, and headed to the well of Las Cruces Diez y Jesús.

The well was there beside the road, with the ten unpainted wooden crosses at one side, and looming behind them under a canopy of plaited branches was the rude, weather-beaten wooden statue of the *Christo*. Ten men had died here beside the lonely road where water offered life to those coming out of the desert. A cross for each life, and the *Christo* watched silently over the spot, mysterious, brooding in the faint starlight.

No one else was there. A coyote howled mournfully in the distance. Leather *creaked* softly as they waited, each man used to the lonely trails and not needing speech.

The first hoof beats they heard were coming from Camargo,

soft, muffled in the road dust.

"*Uno*," Tucker muttered.

"*Sí*," Brent said softly. They were in Mexico and the habits of the country were falling about them as naturally as if they were at the Valle de Taos, by the upper waters of the Río Grande.

The solitary rider reined to a walk, and then to a stop where their forms were visible in the faint starlight.

"*Canales*," Brent said, and he heard a quiet "*Muerto.*"

He rode forward to talk. The rider beckoned and turned back along the road, and in no more than 100 yards wheeled to the left and rode into the chaparral on a narrow trail Brent would hardly have noticed in daylight, and passed in the dark. The other two followed.

It was a rough trail, little traveled. No wagon had ever come this way. Miles were behind them, two full hours had passed before the steadily riding figure pulled into a walk.

"Where do we go?" Brent asked in Spanish, peering at the slender young man who rode silently with hat brim pulled down.

"Ask the devil, *señor*," was the careless answer he got back in Spanish. "He made the trail."

Brent stiffened. He could feel the cold and then the hot crawl of certainty that the voice brought. He rode closer, looking hard at the slender figure riding beside him. His exclamation reached to Tucker and Shorty.

"What the devil is this? Rosita!"

The figure pulled up and swung the dark horse to face the three of them. "Why not?" asked Rosita calmly. She spoke good English and Brent fancied she was amused.

"That gal again?" Tucker blurted.

"We been tricked," Shorty Quade jerked out. "Grab her, Johnny!" Shorty circled out to ride behind her.

"Captain Blandon will not like this," Rosita said, unruffled.

"My orders were to be followed."

Now Brent knew why the captain's grim amusement had persisted. He had an angry, and then a helpless feeling, as if the flood current of war had caught them all up, swirling them on helplessly. The anger he realized was at Captain Blandon for letting this come to pass, for letting this girl ride into the dangerous night, with all decisions in her hand.

"Shorty!" Brent warned. He added: "Blandon evidently knew what he was doing."

"Couldn't have," Tucker Mossby growled.

"*Señor* Blackwhiskers," said Rosita coolly, "be quiet."

Tucker sounded like something was softly strangling down in his wild black beard. It might have been anger or amusement. Tucker fell silent.

"Captain Blandon is not a fool," Rosita said. "There was no other way. Please, if you don't believe that, perhaps we won't come back."

"Blandon shouldn't have let a woman do anything like this," Brent snapped.

"Woman, man, what does it matter?" Rosita said carelessly. "I have the head. You have the guns."

"It's a purty head, to Johnny Brent's way of thinkin'," Shorty observed gravely. "He's been mighty sure you wasn't up to anythin' wrong. How about it, Johnny?"

"Keep quiet."

"A little more talk like that and we return to see what Captain Blandon thinks about it," Rosita said coldly. "He is not a fool. He promised not to send fools with me."

"You win, ma'am," said Shorty with grudging admiration, "We're friends anyway, ain't we? We saved your hair, an' then you saved our hair back there in Matamoras. A man hisself couldn't have done better. Trot out your orders. We're with you."

"Then listen to me," said Rosita slowly. "We are riding all night to the Plaza Ladrones. I know this country better than you know your mountains in the north. My father was a Monterey and Chihuahua trader. His men and his wagons went everywhere, and his pack trains, too, from Chihuahua to Matamoras and San Antonio, in Texas, and as far south as Mexico City. After my mother died, I went with Father everywhere. I know the people, the trails, the *ranchos,* as my father knew them from the time he was a young man. I have friends and enemies. Not everyone liked my father. He was a man. He could take care of himself, and did."

"Is he alive?" Brent asked.

"I don't know. He was arrested in Monterey, by order of General Ampudia. I have heard he was sent to Saltillo under heavy guard, and I have heard he is still in Monterey. Ampudia has offered ten thousand *pesos* if I am brought back to Monterey. That I know. It makes me think father is still alive. Or perhaps not."

"What is your father's name?" Brent asked.

"Michael O'Brien."

"Miguel O'Brien!" Tucker exploded softly in his black beard. "Big Mike O'Brien, of Chihuahua. Lord bless ye, gal. I've heard the wagon men back from Chihuahua to Santa Fé spin tales of Big Mike O'Brien An' the wonderful purty gal he had who was called the Chihuahua Rose. You ain't . . . ?"

"I'm Mike O'Brien's daughter, and we're wasting time," she said crisply, and she wheeled the big dark horse and was away through the night.

Brent spurred and rode beside her, half forgotten scraps of talk out of the past racing through his mind. He was trying to remember something, and he got it.

"Mollie O'Brien!" he called across to her. She looked instinctively, and Brent laughed. "It's a nicer name than Rosita.

What do we find at this Plaza Ladrones?"

"A bullet for a loose mouth and knives for a back without eyes," Mollie O'Brien answered clearly. "I'll thank you to keep your mind on riding, *Señor* Brent. I've no wish to die until I find out about Mike O'Brien,"

Brent marveled that night that a girl could ride so surely through this wild and lonely country. They left the trail and followed the stars across open, broken landscape where tall-armed ocotillo cactus and stately Spanish bayonet and beds of prickly pear grew on the parched ground. The coyotes were with them in the near and far distance; the night chill belied the blazing sun that would hang overhead in a few hours. They passed no water, no ranches; only once did they see the faint glow of a small campfire miles away.

Mollie O'Brien reined to a slow walk, standing in the stirrups as she studied that tiny uncertain red eye in the distance.

"We will ride quietly *poco a poco*," she said softly. "This is the range of Canales, the bandit, and the *rancheros* who are riding with him. They'll slit your throats, *compañeros*, and perhaps decide to sell me to Ampudia . . . and perhaps not. Canales has sworn death to all *los Americanos*."

For half an hour they rode cautiously, and then faster. The feel of dawn was in the east when they came in among small, barren hills. For the first time Mollie O'Brien seemed uncertain. The warning of light was across the stars and the first pale touch of gray on the eastern horizon when Mollie said: "Wait here."

She spurred up the slope to the left and vanished—was gone.

They dismounted, stretching, examining cinches on the tired horses. After some minutes Tucker said: "Some gal."

Brent stood looking up the slope, his thoughts musing on that slender, boyish figure that had come tirelessly over the long miles. She had left many things unsaid, but undoubtedly

Captain Blandon knew what he was doing.

Then dawn was across the sky, and they could look up the rough slope and see the first light strike Mollie O'Brien, sitting her horse just under the crest, looking over and beyond. Tucker nodded approvingly.

"She ain't a squaw, boys, but watch her keep outta sight on the downslope."

Mollie wheeled her horse down to them in cascading dirt and small rocks.

"*Bueno,*" she said, smiling. "Now we will sleep today."

"Then we better find water, ma'am," Tucker warned. "Canteens is low."

"And a fire to cook is dangerous," said Mollie cheerfully. "*Señores,* I am sorry it is hard for you."

Tucker was chuckling as he climbed into the saddle. Brent heard a snort in the black beard. "Sorry for me," Tucker chuckled to himself. "Never seen the beat of her."

That day they slept beside hobbled horses in the shade of a high bank, with the barren hills around and one man taking watch on higher ground. A dry camp, a hard camp, and, before it was Brent's turn to rise and take watch, he stepped softly to Mollie O'Brien and stood looking down at her. She slept quietly in her single blanket, one small firm hand crossed to the opposite shoulder. The brown hair was curly about her damp forehead, and she looked young. Too young to be here.

His gaze must have penetrated her slumber. Eyelids stirred, opened wide at sight of Brent's figure. Then Mollie recognized him, and lay looking at him with sleep-dimmed eyes. The ghost of a smile came on her mouth. The arm shifted up over her eyes and she drew a long, contented breath and went back to sleep.

When the four of them waited beside the saddled horses for the slow twilight to fold in, Mollie O'Brien was unsmiling, earnest as she talked and scratched a crude map in the dirt with a stick.

"We are here. The Plaza of Thieves is here, about ten miles southwest, in those hills you have seen. This man Murphy should be there tonight."

"What is the place?" Brent asked. "A bandit *campo?*"

"Long ago, they say. Now only honest people live there. The best man there is my father's old friend, *Don* Santiago Trujillo, who is not unknown to General Ampudia in Monterey. *Don* Santiago will perhaps go into Monterey with me to ask about my father."

"But Murphy, ma'am?" Tucker Mossby urged impatiently. "What's he doin' here? There's a heap we don't know about that feller an' you an' that business over in Texas. Cap'n Blandon might be satisfied, but I ain't. Dead babies is dead babies. How come you know so much about what this skunk Murphy is doin' now?"

"I think I know Murphy," Mollie said slowly. She poked the stick at the ground and looked as if her mind was back in the thorn brush where the white bones lay in the high grass. "He worked for my father, and stole, and was hurt badly in a terrible fight he had with Father when he was discharged. Since then, he has hated and lived like a bandit. We knew that, because all news came to Miguel O'Brien sooner or later over the trails. In Matamoras, where he fooled Captain Blandon and was spying for Canales, Murphy heard that Miguel O'Brien had sensed war was coming and had sent a large amount of gold north across the Río Grande, to be buried and safe if needed. It was true. The gold was sent in bundles of goatskins in charge of the man my father trusted most. Old Pedro Galego. His wife had been my nurse. They went with the gold to their youngest son's place across the Río Grande and buried it at an agreed spot."

"And Murphy went after it?" Tucker growled.

Mollie nodded. "With scum he had found in the army at

Matamoras. He did not trust his Mexican friends. For gold"—
Mollie drew a finger across her throat and took a long breath. "I
didn't know that when I rode across the river to get away from
Ampudia's reward of ten thousand *pesos*. I needed some of
father's money, and I needed Pedro Gallego's help. A cousin of
old Pedro's guided me. Murphy and his friends found us. I
thought they were Indians at first. They killed Pedro's cousin,
and made me dress like in Indian boy, and turned back with
me. Murphy was sure I knew where the gold was. He wouldn't
believe me when I said I was going to meet a party of my father's
friends at Pedro's place. A large party, all armed."

"Were you?" Brent inquired.

"No. But I tried to pretend. I think it made Murphy cau-
tious. His men were still planning to return as soldiers to Matamoras, with the gold, if possible, divided and hidden again.
They had met a small party of Indians and decided to ride like
Indians, so they'd never be suspected. I did not know where we
were when they met you men. I knew they wanted to be sure
they wouldn't be discovered. They tied me and scattered out in
the brush. The shooting started, and Murphy came running
back and ordered me to ride away with him. You know the rest."

"I don't know why you rode away from me," Brent said.

"Gold is gold," Mollie said, shrugging. "How did I know who
you were? *Señor* Blackwhiskers was not gentle. And when I saw
the bodies and the little blue boots. . . ." Mollie swallowed
hard. "I had bought them myself for Pedro's wife to take to her
little grandsons. Her hair was there! All I could do was ride fast
to get away from everything."

"You showed up in a queer place, ma'am," Shorty reminded.
"When did Chihuahua O'Brien's gal start kickin' her heels in a
cut-throat *cantina?*"

"In Matamoras," Mollie said, smiling again. "That was fun. I
like to dance. Murphy's sweetheart, Polly Morales, did not know

me, or know that I knew who she was, and that she was spying for General Canales. She forgot that all talk reached the O'Briens."

"One of Murphy's men told me before he died that Polly was dancing in Matamoras, and he warned me to watch the Rooster," Brent said. "I still don't understand why he did so."

"A young man with brown hair?"

"Yes."

Mollie punched the dirt with her stick and frowned. "That man listened hard when I accused Murphy of spying for Canales. I don't think he liked it. For gold he would kill, but he was an American. I think perhaps he disliked Murphy after that. But he was with them and could do nothing until he was dying. He had that look all day when his glance was on Murphy. So you knew about Polly Morales? Well, she has been helpful."

"In what way?" Brent countered.

Night was closing fast about them. Mollie O'Brien was becoming a slim and indistinct figure.

"The O'Briens will never be safe while Murphy is alive and knows our money is buried across the Río Grande. It may be the cause of Mike O'Brien's death, if he is still alive. If Murphy can't get that money alone, he'll have help. Canales, Ampudia, a dozen men would like to find it. That red-headed *Gallo* who kills babies would do worse for the money. I know him. So I told Polly Morales where I was going, and Captain Blandon has done the rest."

"Yes?" said Brent.

Her voice came out of the blue-black shadows patiently, almost lightly. "I am on my way to see *Don* Santiago Trujillo, at Thieves' Plaza, and ask him to go into Monterey with me to find news of Miguel O'Brien. Polly Morales left Matamoras quickly after I told her. There has been time for her to talk with

Murphy, and for Murphy to travel to Plaza Ladrones to meet me."

"You ain't sure he's there?" Tucker asked in a disappointed tone.

"I'm sure Polly Morales saw him. I had her followed. The man was found dead, so I know she saw Murphy," Mollie said calmly. "And I know Murphy. That gold has built a fire in his greed that won't go out. He'll be at the plaza to meet you. You'll see. I don't know how many men will be with him. No one knows we are here. I will ride ahead to *Don* Trujillo's house, and you will follow me." Mollie laughed softly. "I am the bait. You are the trap. Murphy is the coyote. ¿*Verdad?*"

"No!" Brent differed hotly. "Tucker, Shorty, are we going to let her? Blandon had no right to let a woman do this!"

"He couldn't stop me," said Mollie defiantly.

"I'd have stopped you. I'd have locked you up."

"You were ordered to do as I say!" Mollie said angrily. She struck the ground with the stick. "Do you think I rode this far to hear such talk? No! Not while Mike O'Brien needs help."

"We'll decide this," Brent told her coldly. "Tucker, how about it?"

Tucker was silent for a moment.

"We jined," Tucker said slowly. "The cap'n made a point of orders. Guess he thinks it's worth the risk. Johnny, I'm ag'in' you."

Mollie O'Brien settled the matter by swinging lightly into the saddle.

"*Don* Santiago lives in the biggest house," she spoke down to them. "His mustache is white and he is fat. You will know him, if necessary. Now I will go first. You will wait where the trail crosses Arroyo Ladrones. If there is no danger in the plaza, I will send a man and you will ride in quietly. If the man does not come in an hour, or if there is a gunshot, Murphy is there."

She spoke the final order in Spanish, almost gaily.

"The rest is with God. *Adiós, compañeros.*"

She rode from them on the big dark horse, and they had to follow to keep her in sight.

IV

Arroyo Ladrones dropped, deep and cruelly scoured, through a steep draw in the harsh and low hills to which they had ridden through the early starlight. The trail dipped down over moist sand in the bottom of the arroyo, angled up the other side steeply, and vanished up the draw. Dogs barked in the direction that Mollie O'Brien had taken. Brent sat restlessly in the saddle, waiting. The distant clamor of coyotes ranged though the lonely vastness behind them.

Brent's comment was an angry breath to the other two: "You were wrong. A man who'll kill old people and young for the feel of money shouldn't have an hour."

"Orders is orders," Tucker muttered uncomfortably.

"Hold my horse and don't wait for me if you need to move," Brent said.

He left them there, and in the damp arroyo sand his feet were mere whispers of sound and he was only a darker blot that advanced through the dark shadows. He came to rock ledges over which he had to climb, once to the height of his chest, and presently the smell of goats and the sweet acrid scent of wood smoke warned that he was near the Plaza Ladrones.

A small place, Mollie O'Brien had said, that had been larger long ago when mines in the mountains not far off were being worked. Brent came up out of the harsh arroyo like a drifting memory. Low walls of sheds and houses lifted before him in the starlight.

The dog that barked to the left, downwind, was not barking at him. The guile of the northern mountains was in his feet and

194

at his nerve tips as he moved between low rock and mud hovels into the open before them.

This was the plaza; he could see the scattering of habitations on either side, with the hills hemming in and the rough trail going out at either end. Eight or ten families, Brent guessed, and the rest only ruins from the past. If he had ridden or walked up the trail, he would have been challenged by the rider who now waited quietly at the lower end of the plaza.

The horse blew and shook its head, *chinking* bit chains softly, and, when Brent drifted a little nearer, he made out the vague silhouette of the rider. While Brent watched, the horse was sent walking slowly on the downtrail. The rider might have been lazily taking word to Tucker and Shorty, could possibly be Mollie O'Brien, and most likely was not.

The peace in Plaza Ladrones was the peace of death, of thieves, bandits long dead. But it was more. Brent resisted fear that an hour was too much to have granted Mollie O'Brien.

She was too young, too reckless; she was still the girl of quick tears over the white hair of her old nurse and the little blue boots she had bought for a child. This business should never have been for her. Sick regret was in the slide of Brent's fingers over the leather haft of his belt knife and the cool hard handle of the Colt revolver. He had left his rifle with Tucker and Shorty, and was glad of it when he stalked the largest building on the plaza and saw tobacco glow like an aroused eye in the doorway.

The house seemed to be without light, but within the thick walls voices stirred faintly as Brent drifted past the corner and came quietly as the night's own hush to the side of the doorway.

The man was still there. The smell of corn shuck smoldering around fragrant tobacco drifted out of the doorway, and then the man whistled softly between his teeth, and turned back inside and opened a door.

"Ain't a stir outside," his voice stated. "You want me to go hustle the boys with the horses?"

"Keep watchin'. I smell somethin' wrong an' don't mean to be surprised."

Brent was a sliding shadow through the doorway as the answer came from deeper in the house. He saw a slit of weak light where the other door was opened, enough light to show the low roof and side walls of the narrow passage that ran through to the back, with rooms on either side. He glimpsed the rifle the man carried as the door closed, and then the blackness was absolute as he stood with shoulders against the mud-plastered stone.

The tobacco glowed again as the man stepped past him toward the doorway. Brent gripped the knife and stepped at his heels, and then in mid-stride Brent switched from knife to heavy Colt gun. He still could shrink from putting steel into an unsuspecting throat while there was another way.

He struck with the gun barrel, hard at the base of the skull, below the hat brim. The meaty *crunch* of metal on bone brought an involuntary grunt from the victim. The rifle *thudded* softly down and the owner collapsed on it.

Brent got knife and revolver off him, rolled the inert figure against the wall, shoved the rifle over beside it, and stepped on back and opened the same door the width of a finger. Spanish was being spoken inside, bitterly.

"You will take her from my house to Monterey for the ten thousand *pesos*, I see. But take me, Santiago Trujillo, her father's friend, with her."

Mollie O'Brien said: "Keep quiet, *Don* Santiago, before there is trouble."

"Never, while I am a man in my own house. I will go to Monterey or. . . ."

Brent heard the dull blow, like the one he had just delivered. Mollie O'Brien cried out in English: "Oh! You didn't have to do that!" Her voice shook. "He's an old man! You've killed him!"

"He ain't the first, lady. We'd sure have had to kill him if he started to Monterey with us." The speaker chuckled. "How about it, Red?"

"I know you aren't taking me to Monterey," Mollie's unsteady voice said. "You men aren't riding to join the San Patricio company as you told him. Murphy has been looking for me."

"Found you, didn't I, honey?" a heavy and amused voice said. "This time we'll ride back across the river and get that money. An' if we don't find it, Ampudia can have you for ten thousand *pesos*. I'd send word to your old man if I knew where he was. He'd pay highest."

"And he'd never stop tracking you down this side of hell!"

"He won't track nobody when I tell General Ampudia how he was working with the Yanks before the war started. Sending reports straight to Washington."

"A lie!"

"Good enough to get O'Brien shot. Since Palo Alto and He saca de la Palma, Yanks don't get coddled in Monterey. I've waited a long time for this, honey. It tastes sweeter every time I chew on it."

"Like a mad cat, ain't she, Red?" the first voice joined in. "Look at her."

"Kill her like a mad cat if she tries to get away," the heavy voice said. "She's Mike O'Brien's daughter, and she'll get us shot yet if she gets the chance. She won't forget."

"No," Mollie said huskily, "I won't forget."

Brent wished she'd stop talking. Every word put her in more danger. He stood by the open slit in the door, wondering how many men Murphy had. There was a man down the road, one on the passage floor behind him, two in there with Mollie. But how many with the horses? How many others out on guard?

Tucker and Shorty were going to be surprised by the guard

when they rode up the trail. Brent was thankful he'd slipped up the arroyo; he was wondering what chance he had to get at Murphy and the other man without danger to Mollie O'Brien, when the decision was taken from him.

Horses trotted to the house; American voices talking carelessly were among the sounds. Then in the direction of Tucker and Shorty gunfire keened sharply.

"Git Murphy!" one of the men outside cried urgently.

Brent stepped into the room.

The light was from three candles flickering in a cluster on a wooden table. The dim light was almost dazzling to Brent's night-widened eyes.

With the first sweeping look he made out a fat, white-haired figure sprawling laxly at the left side of the room. A lanky man with flat-crowned black hat pushed back was turning toward him. Mollie O'Brien's boyish figure was on the other side of the table, and a step beyond her across the candlelight was a big, brutally handsome stranger with a shock of challenging red hair.

They thought at first he was one of them. The light dazzled Murphy's eyes a little, too, perhaps. "Anything wrong out there?" Murphy demanded.

Brent took time to slam the door behind him, and even that slight delay was costly. The lanky man saw trouble and acted without speaking. His gun was drawn and firing as Brent lunged desperately to one side and fired back.

Through the bright muzzle flashes and ear-deafening reports Brent felt the burn of a bullet against his side. He was pulling the trigger again, still moving in the lunge, when a hand slapped all three candles off the table and the low-roofed room was drowned in utter blackness.

"Damn her!" the heavy bellow of Murphy rang out. The table crashed over.

Brent was already down, dodging back the other way as Murphy's gun lashed flame. The lanky man's gun spoke a third time. Brent fired at it and kept moving fast along the floor, and, when both men shot wildly at him, they missed.

Ears could hear little, but the cry that came through the powder reek was audible. "Red! He hit me!"

Murphy did not answer.

"Red!"

Brent fired at the voice and jumped to one side. "Keep flat, Mollie!" he yelled, and kept moving.

She didn't answer. Murphy and his companion fired at the sound of Brent's voice, and Brent shot again at the flash of the lanky man's gun, low down toward the floor.

Brent dared not fire toward Murphy, who seemed to be keeping in that end of the room. Mollie O'Brien had been that way, too. He had the cold anger of helplessness. She had been standing close to Murphy and she did not answer.

Men in the passage jerked the door open.

"What's wrong, Murph? We're in a trap!"

Brent fired at the doorway. A man yelled with pain. Then Murphy's bawl filled the room. "Come in an' help git him! He's used up his six shots! I been countin'!"

Murphy's gun opened fire at the spot where Brent had been. Three shots as fast as Murphy could pull the trigger. One of them drove bits of the hard earthen floor into Brent's face.

He was looking at the doorway, and by the gun flashes behind him he saw the first man fill the doorway in response to Murphy's order. Brent hammered two shots from the gun he had taken off the guard, and kept on going back across the room. Men cursed outside the door.

"What the hell's wrong, Murphy? Was that you? Andy's kilt!"

A second man called angrily: "Are you comin' out, Murph?"

A gun fired out front. A man cried urgently: "They're closin' in! Hurry up!"

"I'm waiting, Murphy," Brent said.

There was no other door out of the room. Murphy would have to pass him, and he knew why the man was silent. Somewhere in the blackness Murphy was waiting, or was slipping toward the door.

Running boots cleared out of the passage. Guns fired again out in the night, close now, as spurred horses started away. In the reeking quiet of the black room Brent took post beside the door and waited, cocked revolver in one hand, knife in the other.

The lanky man had stopped all sound. The quiet of death was over Mollie O'Brien. It was hard to wait, but this was the way it had to be, this was the way Murphy had to come out of the room.

"He's coming on the left side," Mollie's voice gasped from the other end of the room.

Brent swung that way, forgetting that her left as she faced him was his right side. The man came with a desperate rush from that right side. He was almost to the floor when Brent fired at the sound, then a viciously swung chair slammed into his arm and shoulder and drove him back against the wall.

The rip of a knife blade went through his shoulder and the gun misfired as he lunged over against Murphy's rush, the chair dropping beside them.

Brent struck out with his knife hand and blocked another vicious stab. No longer trusting the gun, he clubbed the heavy barrel at the spot where Murphy's face should be. The man stumbled against him, and, when Brent struck again with the gun, Murphy went down heavily.

Panting, Brent bent over him, feeling with a foot for a sign of movement.

"Mollie," he said thickly. "Keep quiet until I get a candle lighted."

Tucker and Shorty found them in candlelight, and Shorty ran back out front to guard and keep out the neighbors who were gathering in the open now that gunfire had stopped.

"Run right smack into a feller on the trail," said Tucker disgustedly. "But I didn't wait fer a whole hour t'be up an' I wasn't sure there was trouble ahead. Johnny, you're bleedin' at the shoulder like a gutted deer."

"I've seen worse," said Mollie O'Brien wanly as she opened the shirt against Brent's protests. "He will be able to ride. And Murphy is still alive."

"That won't be hard to fix," Tucker said, and drew his hunting knife.

"No," Mollie O'Brien said involuntarily. Her eyes were wide as she looked up at Brent. "Not like he is. Not while he's helpless."

"You'd see him carried back to Camargo after all he's done?" Brent asked her.

Mollie swallowed, nodded.

"Tucker," Brent said, "we're still taking orders."

Tucker for once seemed to realize that it had to be like this. "We better git started an' be a long way from here by daylight," he said. "No tellin' what'll be down around our ears if we tarry. Daylight ridin' jes' won't be healthy."

Don Santiago was a sick man, but he was sitting up and reassuring his neighbors when they left on the out trail with Murphy lashed to a horse.

Brent's slashed shoulder hurt, but he was strangely at peace as he rode beside Mollie O'Brien.

"I won't forget this trip, ma'am. But I'll never make another with you. A girl has no place in this sort of business."

Mollie's laugh was still a bit unsteady. "I think I knew that when I hugged the floor and waited to see who would die next. You're all angry at me for taking Murphy back, aren't you?"

"I think we're all glad to see you wanted to take him back," Brent said slowly. "There's not much mercy in the fur country and little enough in war. We expected it in you, ma'am."

She rode in silence for a full minute, and then she said: "No one has ever said a nicer thing to me. I'll remember it if we never meet again."

"We'll meet. Be sure of that, ma'am."

"I wonder," she answered lightly, and dropped back and let him lead the way.

Brent was smiling, that she should doubt they would meet again. He was still thinking of her when Shorty's quirted horse drew up beside him.

"She's gone, Johnny."

Brent brought his horse to a rearing stop. Tucker and the prisoner closed up with them. "Gone where?"

"Said sudden-like to me she's goin' to Monterey to find her father. And not to foller her. Then she was gone off the trail on that big horse like the devil was in her saddle." Shorty swore helplessly. "I didn't know what to do. Wasn't a chance to stop her outside a long chase."

Brent listened. The night already had swallowed any sound Mollie's horse made, and blotted her tracks.

"Johnny, she ain't one to hold," said Tucker dryly. "Don't do it, Johnny. You wouldn't find her tonight . . . an' they're lookin' fer Yank riders between here an' Monterey. Don't try it, Johnny. Orders is orders." And Tucker added the one thing that carried weight: "We'll need you, Johnny, to git this skunk back to Camargo, where the law'll hang him."

"Ride on," Brent said heavily as he lifted the reins. "We'll get him there."

But Brent was looking back in the fathomless night and making plans as he led them on. Off there across the dry, lonely miles, Monterey was waiting for Taylor's army. There would be a way to get there quickly. He had always wanted to see Monterey, and now he knew he was going, and quickly.

ABOUT THE AUTHOR

T. T. Flynn was born Thomas Theodore Flynn, Jr., in Indianapolis, Indiana. He was the author of over 100 Western stories for such leading pulp magazines as Street & Smith's *Western Story Magazine*, Popular Publications' *Dime Western*, and Dell's *Zane Grey's Western Magazine*. He lived much of his life in New Mexico and spent much of his time on the road, exploring the vast terrain of the American West. His descriptions of the land are always detailed, but he used them not only for local color but also to reflect the heightening of emotional distress among the characters within a story. Following the Second World War, Flynn turned his attention to the book-length Western novel and in this form also produced work that has proven imperishable. Five of these novels first appeared as original paperbacks, most notably *The Man from Laramie* (1954) which was also featured as a serial in *The Saturday Evening Post* and subsequently made into a memorable motion picture directed by Anthony Mann and starring James Stewart, and *Two Faces West* (1954) which deals with the problems of identity and reality and served as the basis for a television series. He was highly innovative and inventive and in later novels, such as *Night of the Comanche Moon* (Five Star Westerns, 1995), concentrated on deeper psychological issues as the source for conflict, rather than more elemental motives like greed. Flynn is at his best in stories that combine mystery—not surprisingly, he also wrote detective fiction—with suspense and action in an artful balance.

The psychological dimensions of Flynn's Western fiction came increasingly to encompass a confrontation with ethical principles about how one must live, the values that one must hold dear above all else, and his belief that there must be a balance in all things. The cosmic meaning of the mortality of all living creatures had become for him a unifying metaphor for the fragility and dignity of life itself. *Last Waltz on Wild Horse* will be his next Five Star Western.